James Mercer Garnett

Elene, Judith, Athelstan or the Fight at Brunanburh

And Byrthtnoth or the Fight at Maldon

James Mercer Garnett

Elene, Judith, Athelstan or the Fight at Brunanburh
And Byrthnoth or the Fight at Maldon

ISBN/EAN: 9783744719841

Printed in Europe, USA, Canada, Australia, Japan

Cover: Foto ©Andreas Hilbeck / pixelio.de

More available books at **www.hansebooks.com**

ELENE;

JUDITH;

ATHELSTAN, OR THE FIGHT AT BRUNANBURH;

AND

BYRHTNOTH, OR THE FIGHT AT MALDON:

Anglo-Saxon Poems.

TRANSLATED BY

JAMES M^{c.} GARNETT, M.A., LL.D.,

PROFESSOR OF THE ENGLISH LANGUAGE AND LITERATURE IN THE
UNIVERSITY OF VIRGINIA; TRANSLATOR OF " BÉOWULF."

———∞•••∞———

BOSTON, U.S.A.:
PUBLISHED BY GINN & COMPANY.
1889.

TYPOGRAPHY BY J. S. CUSHING & Co., BOSTON, U.S.A.

PRESSWORK BY GINN & Co., BOSTON, U.S.A.

CONTENTS.

JUDITH.

PREFACE.

THIS translation of the ELENE was made while reading the poem
with a post-graduate student in the session of 1887–88, Zupitza's
second edition being used for the text, which does not differ mate-
rially from that in his third edition (1888). It was completed
before I received a copy of Dr. Weymouth's translation (1888), from
Zupitza's text; but in the revision for publication I have referred to
it, although I cannot always agree with the learned scholar in his
interpretation of certain passages. Grein's text was, however, used
to fill *lacunæ*, and in the revision the recently published (1888)
Grein-Wülker text was compared in some passages. The line-for-
line form has been employed, as in my translation of BÉOWULF;
for it has been approved by high authority, and is unquestionably
more serviceable to the student, even if I have not been able to
attain ideal correctness of rhythm. I plead guilty in advance to
any *lapsus* in that respect, but I strongly suspect that I have appre-
ciated the difficulty more highly than my future critics. The ELENE
is more suitable than the BÉOWULF for first reading in Old English poetry on account of its style and its subject, which make the
interpretation considerably easier, and I concur with Körting, in
his *Grundriss der Geschichte der Englischen Litteratur* (p. 47, 1887):
" Die ELENE eignet sich sowohl wegen ihres anmutigen Inhaltes,
als auch, weil sie in der trefflichen Ausgabe von Zupitza leicht
zugänglich ist, als erste poetische Lectüre für Anfänger im Angelsächsischen." This statement is now the stronger for English

readers because Zupitza's text is in course of publication, edited with introduction, notes, and glossary by Professor Charles W. Kent, of the University of Tennessee. I have appended a few notes which explain themselves, and have occasionally inserted words in brackets.

The translations of the JUDITH and the BYRHTNOTH were made in regular course of reading with undergraduate classes, the former in 1886, and the latter in 1887, the texts in Sweet's "Anglo-Saxon Reader" being used, and compared with those in Grein and in Körner. The text of JUDITH is now accessible in Professor Cook's edition (1888).

The translation of the ATHELSTAN has been added from Körner's text, compared with Grein and Wülker, and in certain passages with Thorpe and Earle. For fuller literary information than the Introduction provides, the reader is referred to ten Brink's "Early English Literature," Kennedy's translation (1883), and to Morley's "English Writers," Vol. II. (1888).

JAMES M. GARNETT.

UNIVERSITY OF VIRGINIA, VA.,
May, 1889.

INTRODUCTION.

Is presenting to the public the following translations of the Old English (Anglo-Saxon) poems, ELENE, JUDITH, ATHELSTAN, and BYRHTNOTH, it is desirable to prefix a brief account of them for the information of the general reader.

I. The ELENE, or Helena, is a poem on the expedition of the Empress Helena, mother of Constantine the Great, the first Christian emperor, to Palestine in search of the true cross, and its successful issue. The mediæval legend of the Finding of the Cross is given in the *Acta Sanctorum* under date of May 4, assigned by the Church to the commemoration of St. Helena's marvellous discovery. The Latin work is the Life of St. Quiriacus, or Cyriacus, Bishop of Jerusalem, that is, the Judas of the poem. It has been usually thought that the Old English poet used this Life as his source ; but Glöde, in a recent volume of *Anglia* (IX. 271 ff.), has given reasons for thinking that the poet used some other Latin text. He rejects ten Brink's conjecture that the legend of Elene had come to England in a Greek form. As to the author of the poem, we know his name, but very little else about him. He has left us his name, imbedded in runic letters as an acrostic, in the last canto of the poem, *q.v.* These letters spell the word CYNE–WULF; but who was Cynewulf? The question is hard to answer, and has given rise to much discussion, which cannot be gone into here. A good summary of it will be found in Wülker's *Grundriss zur Geschichte der Angelsächsischen Litteratur* (p. 147 ff., 1885), an indispensable work for students of Old English literature. The old view, propounded in the infancy of Anglo-Saxon studies, and held by Kemble, Thorpe, and, doubtfully, Wright, that he was the Abbot of Peterborough and Bishop of Winchester (992–1008), has been abandoned by all scholars, so far as I know, except Professor Earle of Oxford (see his " Anglo-Saxon Literature," p. 228). The later view of Leo, Dietrich, Grein and Rieger, our chief authorities, that he was a Northumbrian, and of Dietrich and Grein, that he was Bishop of Lindisfarne (737–780), has more to be said for it. Sweet and ten Brink also hold that he was a Northumbrian of the eighth century, but not the Bishop of Lindisfarne, while Wülker regards him as a West-Saxon. Professor Henry Morley, in the current edition of his " English Writers," has devoted a chapter (Vol. II. Chap. IX., 1888) to Cynewulf, and virtually concludes that we know nothing about him except that he was a poet and probably lived in the eighth century. We shall not go far wrong in regarding him as a Northumbrian poet of the eighth century, possibly the Bishop of Lindisfarne, even though his works remain to us only in the West-Saxon dialect. As in the ELENE, so in the CHRIST and the JULIANA, Cynewulf has left us his name, hence all agree in ascribing to him these poems at least. To these some of the RIDDLES, if not all, are usually added, but this is now contested. Other poems, as the GUTHLAC, PHŒNIX, CHRIST'S DE- SCENT INTO HELL, ANDREAS, DREAM OF THE ROOD, and several other shorter poems, have been ascribed to him with more or less probability, and very recently Sarrazin (in *Anglia*, IX. 515 ff.) would credit him with the authorship of even the BÉOWULF (!). We might as well assign to him, as has been suggested, all the poems in the two great manuscripts, the Exeter Book and the Ver- celli Book, and be done with it. It is desirable that his authorship of the DREAM OF THE ROOD, which ten Brink and Sweet assign to him, but Wülker rejects, should be proved or disproved ; for with this is connected the question of his Northumbrian origin, and some lines from this poem have been inscribed in the Northumbrian dialect on the Ruthwell Cross in Dumfriesshire. However it may be, a poet named Cynewulf wrote the ELENE, and thereby left us one of the finest Old English poems that time has preserved, on a subject that was of great interest to Christian Europe. A collection of "Legends of the Holy Rood" has been issued by the Early English Text Society (ed. Morris, 1871), from the Anglo-Saxon period to Caxton's translation of the *Legenda Aurea*; but they are arranged without system, and no study has been made of the date and relation of the several forms of the story. If Cynewulf made use of the Latin Life of Cyriacus in the *Acta Sanctorum*, he expanded his source considerably and showed great skill and originality in his treatment of the subject, as may be seen by comparing the translation with the Latin text in Zupitza's third edition of the ELENE (1888), or in Professor Kent's forthcoming American edition, after Zupitza. The Old English text was discovered by a German scholar, Dr. F. Blume, at Vercelli, Italy, in 1822, and the manuscript has since become well known as the Vercelli Book (cf. Wülker's *Grundriss*, p. 237 ff.). A reasonable conjecture as to how this MS. reached Vercelli may be found in Professor Cook's pamphlet, "Cardinal Guala and the Vercelli Book." A Bibliography of the ELENE will be found in Wülker, Zupitza, and Kent. English translations have been made by Kemble, in his edition of the Codex Vercellensis (1856), and very recently by Dr. R. F. Weymouth, Acton, England, after Zupitza's text (privately printed, 1888). A German translation will be found in Grein's *Dichtungen der Angelsachsen* (II. 104 ff., 1859), and of lines 1–275 in Körner's *Einleitung in das Studium des Angelsächsischen* (p. 147 ff., 1880). A good summary of the poem is given in Earle's "Anglo-Saxon Literature" (p. 234 ff., 1884), and a briefer one in Morley's "English Writers" (II. 196 ff.).

The ELENE is conceded to be Cynewulf's best poem, and ten

Brink remarks of the ANDREAS and the ELENE: "In these Cynewulf appears, perhaps, at the summit of his art" (p. 58, Kennedy's translation). The last canto is a personal epilogue, of a sad and reflective character, evidently appended after the poem proper was concluded. This may be the last work of the poet, and there is good reason for ten Brink's view (p. 59) that "not until the writing of the ELENE had Cynewulf entirely fulfilled the task he had set himself in consequence of his vision of the cross. Hence he recalls, at the close of the poem, the greatest moment of his life, and praises the divine grace that gave him deeper knowledge, and revealed to him the art of song."

II. The JUDITH is a fragment, but a very torso of Hercules. The first nine cantos, nearly three-fourths of the poem, are irretrievably lost, so that we have left but the last three cantos with a few lines of the ninth. The story is from the apocryphal book of Judith, and the part remaining corresponds to chapters XII. 10 to XVI. 1, but the poet has failed to translate the grand thanksgiving of Judith in the sixteenth chapter. The story of Judith and Holofernes is too well known to need narration. The poet, doubtless, followed the Latin Vulgate, as we have no reason to think that a knowledge of Greek was a common possession among Old English poets; but, as Professor Cook says, "the order of events is not that of the original narrative. Many transpositions have been made in the interest of condensation and for the purpose of enhancing the dramatic liveliness of the story."

The Old English text is found in the same manuscript with the BÉOWULF (Cotton, Vitellius, A, xv.), and, to my mind, this poem reminds the reader more of the vigor and fire of BÉOWULF than does any other Old English poem; but its author is unknown. It has been assigned by some scholars to the tenth century, which is rather late for it; but Professor Cook has given reasons for thinking that it may have been written in the second half of the ninth century in honor of Judith, the step-mother of King Alfred. It was first printed as prose by Thwaites at the close of his "Heptateuch, Book of Job, and Gospel of Nicodemus" (1698), and has been often reprinted, its shortness and excellence making it a popular piece for inclusion in Anglo-Saxon Readers. A most complete edition has been recently (1888) issued by Professor Albert S. Cook, with an excellent introduction, a translation, and a glossary. A Bibliography is given by Professor Cook (pp. 71-73), and by Wülker (*Grundriss*, p. 140 ff.). To the translations therein enumerated may be added the one in Morley's "English Writers" (II. 180 ff.). Professor Cook has also given (pp. lxix-lxxii) the testimonies of scholars to the worth of this poem. To these the attention of the reader is especially called. The JUDITH has been treated by both ten Brink and Wülker as belonging to the Caedmon circle, but the former well says (p. 47): "This fragment produces an impression more like that of the national epos than is the case with any other religious poetry of that epoch;" and Sweet (Reader, p. 157) regards it as belonging "to the culminating point of the Old Northumbrian literature, combining as it does the highest dramatic and constructive power with the utmost brilliance of language and metre."

III. The ATHELSTAN, or Fight at Brunanburh, is found in four manuscripts of the "Anglo-Saxon Chronicle" and in Wheloc's edition (1643), printed from a MS. that was burnt in the unfortunate fire among the Cottonian manuscripts (1731). It is entered under the year 937 in all but one MS., where it occurs under 938. The poem gives a brief, but graphic, description of the fight between King Athelstan and his brother Edmund on the one side, and Constantine and his Scots aided by Anlaf and his Danes, or Northmen, on the other, in which fight the Saxons were completely victorious. The poem will be found in all editions of the "Anglo-Saxon Chronicle" from Wheloc to Earle (1865), and has been repeatedly reprinted, its brevity causing it to be often included as a specimen

of Old English, but it is omitted in Sweet's Reader. A Bibliography will be found in Wülker's *Grundriss* (p. 339 ff.). To the
English translations there mentioned, — which include a poetical
one by Lord Tennyson, after a prose translation by his son in the
Contemporary Review for November, 1876, — may be added the
prose translation by Kennedy in ten Brink (p. 91) and the rhyth-
mical one by Professor Morley in his "English Writers" (II. 316–
17). ten Brink thinks that the poem was not written by an eye-
witness, and says (p. 92): "The poem lacks the epic perception
and direct power of the folk-song as well as invention. The
patriotic enthusiasm, however, upon which it is borne, the lyrical
strain which pervades it, yield their true effect. The rich resources
derived from the national epos are here happily utilised, and the
pure versification and brilliant style of the whole stir our admira-
tion." It well serves to diversify and enliven the usually dry
annals of the "Anglo-Saxon Chronicle," and cannot be spared in
the great dearth of poetry of this period.   •

IV. The BYRHTNOTH, or Fight at Maldon, relates in vigorous
verse the contest between the Saxons, led by the Ealdorman Byrhtnoth, and the Danes at the river Panta, near Maldon in Essex, in
which the Danes were victorious and Byrhtnoth was slain. The
incident is mentioned in four manuscripts of the "Anglo-Saxon
Chronicle" under the year 991, but one gives it under 993. The
MS. in which the poem was contained was unfortunately burnt
in the great fire above-mentioned (1731); but Thomas Hearne, the
antiquary, had fortunately printed it, as prose, in his edition of
the Chronicle of John of Glastonbury (1726); hence this is now
our sole authority for the text, which is defective at both the beginning and the end. The poem has been highly esteemed by
scholars, and is a very valuable relic of late tenth century literature. It has been often reprinted, and translated several times in
whole or in part. Grein does not translate either the ATHELSTAN

or the BYRHTNOTH. Körner translates it in full, and so does
Zernial in his Program "Das Lied von Byrhtnoth's Fall" (1882).
This monograph contains the fullest study of the poem that has
been made. It is translated into English, with some omissions,
by Kennedy in ten Brink (pp. 93–96); it is barely mentioned by
Earle (p. 147), and a summary of it is given by Morley in "English Writers" (II. 319–320). A Bibliography will be found in
Wülker's *Grundriss* (pp. 344–5). An edition of both ATHELSTAN
and BYRHTNOTH has been long announced in the "Library of
Anglo-Saxon Poetry," but it has not yet appeared. Sweet says of
the BYRHTNOTH (Reader, p. 138): "Although the poem does
not show the high technical finish of the older works, it is full of
dramatic power and warm feeling;" and ten Brink, with more enthusiasm, calls it (p. 96) "one of the pearls of Old English poetry,
full, as it is, of dramatic life, and fidelity of an eye-witness. Its
deep feeling throbs in the clear and powerful portrayal." He
recognizes, however, "the tokens of metrical decline, of the disso-
lution of ancient art-forms."

This brief Introduction will, it is hoped, be sufficient to interest
the reader in the accompanying translations of some of the finest
pieces of Old English poetry that remain to us from the eighth,
ninth, and tenth centuries. The earlier period was the golden age
of Old English poetry in the Northumbrian dialect, which poetry,
there is good reason to think, was copied into the West-Saxon·
dialect, and it now remains to us only in that form; for when
the Northmen harried Northumbria, destroyed its monasteries,
massacred its inhabitants, and settled in its homes, manuscripts
perished, and the light of learning in Western Europe was extin-
guished. It is sufficient to recall King Alfred's oft-quoted lament,
in the Preface to his translation of Pope Gregory's "Pastoral
Care," to realize the position held by Northumbria in respect to
culture, and when learning was restored in Wessex by the efforts

of the king himself, and poetry again revived, it shone but by a reflected light. Still we should treasure all that remains, and the Old English language should be at least as well known as Latin is now, and should occupy as prominent a position in education and general culture. Until that millennial period arrives, translations of Old English poems may not be without service.

———

ABBREVIATIONS IN NOTES.

C. = Cook;   Gm. = Grimm;   Gn. = Grein;   Kr. = Körner;
Sw. = Sweet;   Th. = Thorpe;   Z. = Zupitza;   Zl. = Zernial.

CYNEWULF'S ELENE.

Whén had elapsed in course of years
Two hundred and three, reckoned by number,
And thirty alsó, in measure of time,
Of winters for th' world, since mighty God
Became incarnate, of kings the Glory,   5
› Upón mid-earth in human form,
Light of the righteous; then sixth was the year
Of Constantine's imperial sway,
Since hé o'er the realm of the Roman people,
The battle-prince, as ruler was raised.   10
The ward of his folk, skilful with shield,
Was gracious to earls.   Strong grew the ætheling's[1]
Might 'neath the heavens.   Hé was true king,
War-keeper of men.   God him strengthened
With honor and might, that to many became he   15
Throughoút this earth to men a joy,
To nations a vengeance, when weapon he raised
Against his foes.   Him battle was offered,
Tumult of war.   A host was assembled,
Folk of the Huns and fame-loving Goths;   20
War-brave they went, the Franks and the Hugs.[2]
Bold were the men [in battle-byrnies, Gn.],
Ready for war.   Bright shone the spears,

---

[1] Prince's.   [2] MS. ' *Huns*,' but Z. reads ' *Hugs*,'   *Cf.* W.

The ringéd corselets.   With shouts and shields
They hoisted the standards.   The heroes were there   25
Plainly assembled, and [host, Gn.] all together.
The multitude marched.   A war-song howled
The wolf in the wood, war-secret concealed not;
The dew-feathered eagle uplifted his song
On the trail of his foes.   Hastened quickly   30
O'er cities of giants[1] the greatest of war-hosts
In bands to battle, such as king of the Huns
Of dwellers-around anywhere might,
Of city-warriors, assemble to war.
Went greatest of armies, — the footmen were
      strengthened   35
With chosen bands, — till in foreign land
The fighters-with-darts upón the Danube's
Bank were encamping, the brave in heart,
'Round the welling of waters, with tumult of host.
The realm of the Romans they wished to oppress,   40
With armies destroy.   Thére was Huns' coming
Known to the people.   Then bade the Cæsar
Against the foes his comrades in war
'Neath arrow-flight in greatest haste
Gather for fight, form battle-array   45
The heroes 'neath heavens.   The Romans were,
Men famed for victory, quickly prepared
With weapons for war, though lesser army
Had théy for the battle than king of the Huns.[2]
They rode 'round the valiant: then rattled the shield,   50
The war-wood clanged: the king with host marched,
With army to battle.   Aloft sang the raven,
Dark and corpse-gréedy.   The band was in motion.

---

[1] 'O'er land of Burgundians,' Gn.
[2] Z. has no point, W. puts (;), Gn. (.)

The horn-bearers blew,[1] the heralds called,
Steed stamped the earth. The host assembled   55
Quickly for contest. The king was affrighted,
With terror disturbed, after the strangers,
The Huns' and Hreths' hóst they[2] observed,
That it[3] on the Romans' kingdom's border
'Round the bank of the river a band assembled,   60
A countless crowd. Heart-sorrow bore
The Romans' ruler, of realm he hoped not
For want of force; had warriors too few,
Trusty comrades, 'gainst th' overmight
Of the brave for battle. The army encamped,   65
The earls 'round the ætheling nigh to the river
In neighboring plain a night-long time,
After force of their foes they first beheld.
Thén in his sleep was shown to him,
To the Cæsar himself where he slept 'mid his men,   70
By the victory-famed seen, a vision of dream.
Effulgent it seemed him, in form of a man,
White and hue-bright, some one of heroes
More splendid appeared than ere or since
He saw 'neath the heavens. From sleep he awaked   75
With boar-sign bedecked. The messenger quickly,
Bright herald of glory, to him made address
And called him by name (the night-veil vanished):
"To thee, Constantine, bade King of the angels,
Wielder of fates, his favor grant,   80
The Lord of Hosts. Fear not for thyself,
Though thee the strangers threaten with terror,
With battle severe. Look thou to heaven,
To the Lord of glory: there help wilt thou find,
A token of victory." Soon was he ready   85

---

[1] 'Hurried,' Z.[3]   [2] 'He,' W.   [3] 'Which,' Z.

At hest of the holy, his heart-lock unloosed,
Upwards he looked as the messenger bade him,
Trusty peace-wéaver. He saw bright with gems
Fair rood of glory o'er roof of the clouds
Adorned with gold: the jewels shone,   90
The glittering tree with letters was written
Of brightness and light: "With this beacon thou
On the dangerous journey [1] wilt the foe overcome,
The loathly host let." The light then departed,
Ascended on high, and the messenger too,   95
To the realm of the pure. The king was the blither
And freer from sorrow, chieftain of men,
In thoughts of his soul, for thát fair sight.

II.

Bade then a likeness [2] defender of æthelings,
Ring-giver of heroes, to that beacon he saw,   100
Leader of armies, that in heaven before
To him had appeared, with greatest haste
[Bade] Constantine [like] the rood of Christ,
The glorious king, a token make.
He bade then at dawn with break of day   105
His warriors rouse and onset of battle,
The standard raise, and that holy tree
Before him carry, 'mid host of foes
God's beacon bear. The trumpets sang
Aloud 'fore the hosts. The raven rejoiced, [3]   110
The dew-feathered eagle beheld the march,
Fight of the fierce ones, the wolf raised his howl,
The wood's frequenter. War-terror arose.

---

[1] 'In the terrible danger,' Gn.   [2] Lit. 'in like manner,' adv.
[3] Add 'at the work.'

There was shattering of shields and mingling of men,
Heavy handstroke and felling of foes,   115
After in arrow-flight first they had met.
On the fated folk showers of darts,
Spears over shields into hosts of foes,
Sword-fierce foemen battle-adders
With force of fingers forwards impelled.   120
The strong-hearted stepped, pressed onwards at once,
Broke the shield-covers, thrust in their swords,
Battle-brave hastened.   Then standard was raised,
Sign 'fore the host, song of victory sung.
The golden helmet, the spear-points glistened   125
On field of battle.   The heathen perished,
Peaceless they fell.   Forthwith they fled,
The folk of the Huns, when that holy tree
The king of the Romans bade raise on high,
Fierce in the fight.   The warriors became   130
Widely dispersed.   Some war took away;
Some with labor their lives preserved
Upon that march; some half-alive
Fled to the fastness and life protected
Behind the stone-cliffs, held their abode   135
Around the Danube; some drowning took off
In the stream of the river at the end of their life.
Then was of the proud ones the force in joy;
They followed the foreigners forth until even
From break of day.   The ash-darts flew,   140
Battle-adders.   The heap was destroyed,[1]
Shield-band of foes.   Very few came
Of the host of the Huns home again thence.
Then it was plain that victory gave
To Constantine the King Almighty   145

---

[1] 'Diminished,' Gn.

In the work of that day, glorious honor,
Might 'neath the heavens, through the tree of his rood.
Went helmet of hosts home again thence,
In booty rejoicing (the battle was ended),
Honored in war.   Came warriors' defence   150
With band of his thanes to deck the strong shield,[1]
War-renowned king, to visit his cities.
Bade warriors' ward the wisest men
Swiftly to synod, who wisdom's craft
Through writings of old had learnt to know,   155
Held in their hearts counsels of heroes.
Then thát gan inquire chief of the folk,
Victory-famed king, throughout the wide crowd,
If any there were, elder or younger,
Who him in truth was able to tell,   160
Make known by speech, what the god were,
The giver of glory,[2] "whose beacon this was,
That seemed me so sheen, and saved my people,
Brightest of beacons, and gave to me glory,
War-speed against foes, through that beautiful tree."   165
They him any answer at all were unable
To give in reply, nor could they full well
Clearly declare of that victory-sign.
Thén did the wisest speak out in words
Before the armed host, that Heaven-king's   170
Token it was, and of that was no doubt.
When they that heard who in baptism's lore
Instructed had been, light was their mind,
Rejoicing their soul, though of them there were few,
That they 'fore the Cæsar might dare to proclaim   175
The gift of the gospel, how the spirits' Defence,
In form of the Trinity worshipped in glory,

---

[1] i.e., with precious stones. Kr. reads ' (rattled strong shields).'
[2] 'Gold,' Kr. 'Lord of the house,' Gn. *Cf.* W.

Incarnate became, Brightness of kings, —
And how on the cross was God's own Son
Hanged 'fore the hosts with hardest pains;   180
The Son men saved from the bonds of devils,
Sorrowful spirits, and a gift to them gave
Through thát same sign that appeared to him
Before his own eyes the token of victory
'Gainst onset of nations; and how the third day   185
From out of the tomb the Glory of heroes,
From death, arose, the Lord of all
The race of mankind, and to Heaven ascended.
So with cunning of mind in secrets of soul
They said to the victor as they by Sylvester[1]   190
Instructed had been.   From him the folk-chief
Baptism received, and continued to hold it
For the time of his days at the will of the Lord.

III.

Thén was in bliss the giver of treasure,
The battle-brave king.   To him was new joy   195
Inspired in his soul; greatest of comforts
And highest of hopes was heaven's Defence.
Then gan he God's law by day and by night
Through gift of the Spirit with zeal proclaim,
And truly himself devoted he eagerly,   200
Gold-friend of men, to the service of God,
Spear-famed, unfaltering.   Then found the ætheling,
Defence of his folk, through learned men,[2]
War-brave, spear-bold. in books of God,
Whére had been hanged with shouts of the host   205
On tree of the rood the Ruler of heaven

---

[1] The Bishop of Rome.   [2] Lit., 'smiths of lore.'

Through envy and hate, just ás the old fiend
Misled with his lies, the people deceived,
The race of the Jews, so that God himself
They hanged, Lord of hosts: hence in misery shall they   210
For ever and ever punishment suffer.
Then praise of Christ by the Cæsar was
In the thoughts of his mind[1] always remembered
For that great tree, and his mother he bade
Gó on a journey with a band of men   215
To [land of] the Jews, earnestly seek
With host of warriors where that tree of glory
Holy 'neath earth hidden might be,
The noble King's rood.   Helena would not
On that expedition be slow to start,   220
Nor that joy-giver's command neglect,
Her own [dear] son's, but soon she[2] was ready
For the wished-for journey, as the helmet of men,
Of mail-clad warriors, her had commanded.
Gan then with speed the crowd of earls   225
Hasten to ship.[3]   The steeds of the sea
'Round the shore of the ocean ready were standing,
Cabled sea-horses, at rest on the water.
Then plainly was known the voyage of the lady,
When the welling of waves she sought with her folk.   230
There many a proud one at Wendel-sea
Stood on the shore.   They severally hastened
Over the mark-paths, band after band,
And then they loaded with battle-sarks,
With shields and spears, with mail-clad warriors,   235
With men and women, the steeds of the sea.
Then they let o'er the billows the foamy ones go,
The high wave-rushers.   The hull oft received

---

[1] Z. supposes *lacuna* of one verse; W. thinks it unnecessary.
[2] Lit., 'the woman.'   [3] Lit., 'to the sea,' or 'sea-journey.'

O'er the mingling of waters the blows of the waves.
The sea resounded. Not since nor ere heard 1   240
On water-stream a lady lead,
On ocean-street, a fairer force.
There might he see, who that voyage beheld,
Burst o'er the bath-way the sea-wood, hasten
'Neath swelling sails, the sea-horse play,   245
The wave-floater sail. The warriors were blithe,
Courageous in mind; queen joyed in her journey.
After to haven the ringèd-prowed
O'er the sea-fastness had finished their course
To the land of the Greeks, they let the keels   250
At the shore of the sea beat by-the breakers,
The old sea-dwellings at anchor fast,
On the water await the fate of the heroes,
When the warlike queen with her band of men
Over the east-ways should seek them again.   255
There wás on [each] earl easily seen
The braided byrnie and tested sword,
Glittering war-weeds, many a helmet,
Beautiful boar-sign. The spear-warriors were,
Men 'round victor-queen, prepared for the march,   260
Brave war-heroes. They marched with joy
Into land of the Greeks, the Cæsar's heralds,
Battle-warriors with armor protected.
There wás to be seen treasure-gem set
'Mid that army-host, gift of their lord.   265
[Then] wás the blessed Helena mindful,
Bold in her thought, of the prince's will,
Eager in mind, in that shé of the Jews,
O'er the army-fields with tested band
Of warriors-with-shields, the land was seeking,   270
With host of men; so it after befell
In little while that thát force of men,

War-famed heroes, to Hierusalem [1]
Came to the city the greatest of crowds,
Spear-famed earls, with the noble queen.   275

IV.

Bade she then order the dwellers-in-city
Most skilled in lore, those far and wide
Among the Jews, each one of men,
For council-talk in meeting to come,
Whó most deeply the secrets of God   280
By righteous law were able to tell.
Then was assembled from distant ways
No little crowd who Moses' law
Were able to tell.   In number there were
Of thousands three·of thóse [learned] men   285
Chosen for lore. The lovely woman
The men of the Hebrews with words gan address:
"I thát most surely have learnt to know
Through secret words of prophets [of old]
In the books of God, that in days of yore   290
Ye worthy were of the glorious King,
Dear to the Lord and daring in deed.
Lo!·yé that wisdom [very, Gn.] unwisely,
Wrongly, rejected, when him ye condemned
Who you from the curse through might of his glory,   295
From torment of fire, thought to redeem,
From fetters' force. Ye filthily spat
On hís fair face who light of the eyes
From blindness [restored], a remedy brought
To you anew by that noble spittle,   300
And often preserved you fróm the unclean

---

[1] A.-S. form retained for the sake of the accent and alliteration.

Spirits of devils. This one to death
Ye gan adjudge, who self from death
Many awakened 'mong host of men
Of your own race to the former life.   305
So blinded in mind ye gan conjoin
Lying with truth, light with darkness,
Hatred with mercy, with evil thoughts
Ye wickedness wove; therefore the curse
You guilty oppresses. The purest Might   310
Ye gan condemn, and have lived in error,
In thoughts benighted, until this day.
Go ye now quickly, with prudence select
Men firm in wisdom, crafty in word,
Who yóur own law, with excellence skilled,   315
In thoughts of their minds most thoroughly have,
Who to me truly are able to say,
Answer to tell for you hencefórth
Of each one of tokens that Í from thee seek."
They went then away sorry-in-mind,   320
The law-clever earls, oppressed with fear,
Sad in their grief, earnestly sought
The wisest men in secrets of words,
That they to the queen might answer well
Both of good and of ill, as shé from them sought. 325
Then théy 'mong the host a thousand of men
Found clever in mind whó the old story
Among the Jews most readily knew.
Then they pressed in a crowd where in pomp awaited
On kingly throne the Cæsar's mother,[1]   330
Stately war-queen with gold adorned,
Helena spake and said 'fore the earls:

---

[1] Lit., 'kinswoman.' The Elizabethan 'Kesar' would preserve the alliteration in this line.

"Hear, clever in mind, the holy secret,
Word and wisdom. Lo! yé the prophets'
Teaching received, hów the Life-giver   335
In form of a child incarnate became,
Ruler of might. Of him Moses sang
And spake this [word],[1] warden of Israel:
'To yóu shall be born a child in secret
Renowned in might, though his mother shall nót   340
Be filled with fruit through love of a man.'
Of him David the king a kingly psalm sang,
The wise old sage, father of Solomon,
And spake thif word, prince of warriors:
'The God of creation before me I saw,   345
Lord of victories. He wás in my sight,
Ruler of hosts, upon my right hand,
Guardian of glory. Thence turn I nót
Ever in life my countenance from him.'[2]
So it again of you Isaiah   350
'Fore the people, the prophet, foretold in words,
Thinking profoundly by spirit of the Lord:
'I raised upon high sons young in years,
And children begat, to whom glory I gave,
Heart-comfort holy: but théy me rejected,   355
With enmity hated, forethought possessed not,
Wisdom of mind, and the wretched cattle,
That on each day one drives and strikes,
Their well-doer know, not at áll with revenge
Bear hate to their friends who give them fodder.   360
And the folk of Israel never were willing
Me to acknowledge, though many for them, ·
In worldly course, of wonders I wrought.'[3]

---

[1] Gn. and Z. W. omits.   [2] Psalms xvi. 8, 9.   [3] Isaiah i. 2, 3.

V.

" Lo! that we heard through holy books,
That the Lord to you gave blameless glory,   365
The Maker, mights' Speed, to Moses said
How the King of heaven ye should obey,
His teaching perform.   Of that ye soon wearied,
And counter to right ye had contended;
Ye shunned the bright Creator of all,   370
The Lord [of Lords],[1] and followed error
'Gainst right of God.   Now quickly go
And find ye still who writings of old
Through craft of wit the best may know,
Your books of law, that answer to me   375
Through prudent mind they may return."
Went then with a crowd depressed in mind
The proud in heart, as thém the queen bade.
Found they five hundred of cunning men,
Chosen comrades, who craft of lore   380
Through memory of mind the most possessed,
Wisdom in spirit.   They back to the hall
In little while again were summoned,
Wards of the city.   The queen them gan
With words address (she glanced over all):   385
" Often ye silly actions performed,
Accursèd wretches, and writings despised,
Lore of your fathers, ne'er more than now,
When ye of your blindness the Healer rejected,
And ye contended 'gainst truth and right,   390
That in Bethlehem the child of the Ruler,
The only-born King, incarnate was,

---

[1] Gn., Z., W.

The Prince of princes. Though the law ye knew,
Words of the prophets, ye wére not then willing,
Workers of sin, the truth to confess."   395
With one mind then they answered her:
"Lo! wé the Hebrew law have learned,
That in days of old our fathers knew,
At the ark of God, nor know we well
Why thou so fiercely, lady, with us   400
Hast angry become. We know not the wrong
That wé have done amid this nation,
Chiefest of crimes [1] against thee ever."
Helena said and 'fore the earls spake
Without concealment; the lady proclaimed   405
Aloud for the hosts: "Now go ye quickly,
Seek out apart who wisdom with you
Might and mindcraft the most may have,
That each of the things they boldly may tell me,
Without delay, that I from them seek."   410
Went they then from the council as the mighty queen,
Bold in the palace, them had commanded,
Sorry-in-mind eagerly searched they,
With cunning sought, what were the sin
That they in the folk might have committed   415
Against the Cæsar, for which the queen blames them.
Then there 'fore the earls óne them addressed,
Cunning in songs (his name was Judas),
Crafty in word: "I surely know,
That she will seek of the victor-tree   420
On which once suffered the Ruler of nations
Free from all faults, own Son of God,
Whom though guiltless [2] of every sin
Through hatred hanged upon the high tree

---

[1] So W. 'Wrongs have committed,' Gm., Gn. and Z. [?]   [2] W.

In days of old oúr own fathers.   425
That was terrible thought.   There is now great need
That we with firmness strengthen our minds,
That we of this murder become not informers,
Where the holy tree was hidden away
After the war-storm, lest máy be rejected   430
The wise old writings and óf our fathers
The lore be lost.   Not long will it be [1]
That of Israelites the noble race
Over the mid-earth may reign any more,
The law-craft of earls, if this be revealed: 435
That same long ago mine elder father
Victory-famed said (his name was Zácchaéus),
The wise old man, to mine own father,
[Who afterwards made it known to his, Gn.] [2] son,
(He went from this world), and spake this word: 440
' If to thée that happen in the days of thy life,
That thou may'st hear of that holy tree
Wise men inquire and questionings raise
Of that victor-wood on which the true King
Was hanged on high, Guardian of heaven,   445
Child of all peace, then quickly declare it,
Mine own dear son, ere death thee remove.
Ne'er may after that the folk of the Hebrews,
The wise in counsel, their kingdom hold,
Rule over men, but *their* fame shall live   450
And their dominion [be glorified ever, Gn.],
To world of worlds with joy be filled,
Who the King that was hanged honor and praise.'

---

[1] Add 'after that.'   [2] *Lacuna* in MS., emended by Gn.

VI.

"Then quickly I to mine own father,
The old law-sage, answer returned: 455
'How might that happen on kingdom of earth
That they on the holy their hands should lay
For reaving of life, our own fathers,
Through hostile mind, if they ere knew
That he were Christ, the King in heaven,   460
True son of Creator, Saviour of souls.'
Then to mé mine elder answer returned,
Wise in his mind my father replied:
'Perceive, young man, the might of God,
The name of the Saviour. That is to each man   465
Unutterable. Him may no one
Upon this earth [ever] find out.
Never that plan that this people framed
Was I willing to follow, but I always myself
Held aloof from their crimes, by no means wrought
    shame   470
To mine own spirit. To them earnestly often
On account of their wrong I made opposition,
When the learned-in-lore counsel were taking,
Were seeking in soul how the Son of their Maker,
Men's Helm,[1] they might hang, the Lord of all,   475
Both angels and men, noblest of children.
They might not so foolish death fasten on him,
Miserable men, as they ere weened,
Afflict with pains, though he for a time
Upon the cross his spirit gave up,   480
Victor-child of God. Then afterwards was

---

[1] i.e., 'defence, protector.'

Raised from the rood the Ruler of heavens,
Glory of all glories, three nights after
Within the tomb was he abiding
Under the darkness, and then on third day,   485
Light of all light, he living arose,
Prince of angels, and he to his thanes,
True Lord of victories, himself revealed,
Bright in his fame.   Then did thy brother
In time receive the bath of baptism,   490
Enlightening belief.   For love of the Lord
Was Stephen then with stones assailed,
Nor ill gave for ill, but for foes of old
Patient implored, prayed King of glory
That he the woe-deed would not lay to their charge, 495
In thát through hate the innocent One,
Guiltless of sins, by the teachings of Saul
They robbed of life, as he through enmity
To misery many of the folk of Christ
Condemned, to death.   Yet later the Lord   500
Mercy him showed, that to many became he
Of people for comfort, when the God of creation,
Saviour of men, had changed his name,
And afterwards he the holy Paul
Was called by name, and no one than he   505
Of teachers of faith, [no] other, was better
'Neath roof of heaven afterwards ever
Of those man or woman brought into the world,
Although he Stephen with stones them bade
Slay on the mountain, thine own brother.   510
Now may'st thou hear, mine own dear son,
How gracious is the Ruler of all,
Though we transgression 'gainst hím oft commit,
The wound of sins, if we soon after
For those misdeeds repentance work   515

Ánd from unrighteousness afterwards cease.
Therefore I truly, and my dear father,
After believed [in the Giver of life, Gn.],
That he had suffered, God of all glories,
Leader of life, painful penalty   520
For mighty need of the race of men.
Therefore I teach thee through secret of song,
My dearest child, that scornful words,
Hatred or blasphemy, never thou work,
Fierce contradiction 'gainst the Son of God.   525
Then wilt thou merit that thee life eternal,
Best of rewards, shall be given in heaven.'
Thus mine own father in days of old
Me unwaxen with words did teach,
Instruct with true speech (his name was Simon),   530
Man wise in words.   Now well do ye know
What of that in your thought may seem to you best
Plainly to tell, if us this queen
Shall ask of that tree, now mine own mind
And thought of heart ye [well] do know."   535
Him then in reply the cleverest of all
In the crowd of men with words addressed:
"Ne'er did we hear any of men
Among this folk save thee just now,
Another thane; declare in this manner   540
Of so secret event.   Do as [best] seems thee,
Thou wise in old lore, if thou be questioned
'Mong the host of men.   Of wisdom has need,
Of wary words and sage's cunning,
Who shall to the noble one answer return   545
Before such a host among the assembly."

VII.

Words waxed in speech; men counsel took
On every side; some hither, some thither,
Considered and thought. Then came many thanes
To the people's assembly. The heralds called,   550
The Cæsar's criers : " This queen you invites,
Men, to the hall, that the council-decisions
Ye rightly may tell. Of rede have ye need
In the place of assembly, of wisdom of mind."
Ready they were, the sad-in-mind   555
People's protectors, whén they were summoned
Through stern command; to court they went
Craft's might to tell. Then gan the queen
The Hebrew men in words address,
Ask the life-weary of writings of old,   560
How ere in the world the prophets sang,
Men holy in spirit, of the Son of God,
Where the Prince [of the people] his sufferings bore,
True son of Creator, for love of souls.
Stubborn they were, harder than stone,   565
Would not that secret rightly make known
Nor answer to her any would tell,
Anger-provokers, of what she sought,
But they of each word made a denial,
Firm in their minds, of what she gan ask,   570
Said that in life they any such thing
Nor ere nor since ever had heard of.
Helena spake and angrily said :
" I [now] in truth to you will say, —
And of this in your life there shall be no deception, —   575
If ye in this falseness longer continue
With treacherous lying, who stand here before me,

That you on the mountain bale-fire shall take,
Hottest of war-waves, and your corpses consume,
The lambent flame, so for you shall that lie   580
To leaving of life [surely] be turned.
Ye may not prove that word, which ye just now in
    wrong
Concealed 'neath heaps[1] of sins. Nor may ye hide
    that fate,
Obscure its deepest might."   In thought of death
    they were
Of pyre and life's end, and delivered then one   585
Well-skilled in songs (to him the name Judas
Was given 'fore kinsmen); — him they gave to the
    queen,
Said of him very wise: "He may truth to thee tell,
Fate's secrets reveal, as thou askest in words,
The law from beginning forth to the end.   590
He is before earth of noble race,
Wise in word-craft and son of a prophet,
Bold in council.   To him 'tis inborn
That he the answers clever may have,
Knowledge in heart.   He to thee shall declare   595
'Fore the crowd of men the gift of wisdom
Through mickle might, as thy mind desires."
In peace she permitted each one to seek
His own [dear] home, and him alone took,
Judas, as hostage, and earnestly prayed   600
That he of the rood would rightly teach,
Which of old in its bed was long concealed,
And she himself apart to her called.
Helena spake to him alone,
Glory-rich queen: "For thee two are ready,   605

---

[1] Lit., 'under the lap (or bosom) of sins.'

Or life or death, as liefer shall be
To thee to choose.   Now quickly declare
To which of the two thou wilt agree."
Judas to her spake again (he might not the sorrow
    avoid,
Avert the ire of the empress.[1]   In the power of the
    queen was he) :   610
"How may him befall who out on the waste,
Tired and foodless, treads the moorland,
Oppressed with hunger, and bread and stone
Both in his sight together[2] shall be,
The hard and the soft, that he take the stone   615
For hunger's defence, care nót for the bread, .
Return to want and reject the food,
Renounce the better, if both he enjoys ? "

VIII.

To him then the blessed answer returned,
Helena 'fore earls without concealment: 620
" If thou in heaven willest to have
Dwelling with angels and life on earth,
Reward in the skies, tell me quickly
Where rests the rood of the King of heaven
Holy 'neath earth, which yé now long   625
Through sin of murder from men have concealed."
Judas replied (his mind was sad,
Heat in his heart and woe for both,
Whether hope of heaven with [all] his soul
He should renounce, along with his present   630

---

[1] MS. *rex* (Latin ?), Z.; ' oppression of care ' (*cearces*), Gn.; ' of hunger '
(*reaces*), Gm.; ' of smoke ' (*rêces*), Schubert; *rex* = *cyninges*, Sievers and W.
[2] Z.

Kingdom 'neath skies, or show the rood):
" How may I that find that long ago happened
In course of winters ?   Now many are gone,
Two hundred or more, reckoned by number;
I may not recount, now the number I know not.   635
Now many have since departed this life,
Of wise and good who wére before us,
Of clever men.   In youth was I
In later days afterwards born,
A child in years.   I cannot what I know not   640
Find in my heart that so long ago happened."
Helena spake to him in answer:
" How has it happened among this people,
That ye so much in mind retain,
Each one of all signs, just as the Trojans   645
In fight effected ?   'Twas greater terror,[1]
Well-known old war, than this noble event,
In course of years.   Ye thát can well
Quickly recount, how many there were
In number of men in that murderous fight   650
Of throwers-with-darts fallen in death
Under the shield-hedge.   Ye have the graves
Under the stone-slopes, and likewise the places
And the number of winters in writings set down."
Judas replied (great sorrow he bore):   655
" That work of war, we, lady mine,
Through direful need remember well,
And that tumult of war in writing set down,
The bearing of nations, but this one never
By ány mán's mouth have we heard   660
Made known to men except here now."
The noble queen gave answer to him:

---

[1] Or, 'war,' Gn.; ' further off,' Gm.

"Thou resistest too much both truth and right
Of the tree of life, and now little before
Thou truly said'st of that victor-tree   665
To thine own people, and now turn'st to a lie."
To her Judas said that he spake that in sorrow
And doubt extreme, worse evil expected.
Him quickly answered the Cæsar's mother :
"Lo! that have we heard through holy books   670
Made known to men that there was hanged
On Calvarý the King's free child,
God's Spirit-son. Thou fully shalt
Wisdom reveal, as writings tell,
About the plain, where the place may be,   675
That Calvarý, ere misery take thee,
Death for thy sins, that I afterwards may
Purify ít at the will of Christ,
For help to men, that holy God,
Almighty Lord, the thought of my heart   680
My wish may fulfil, men's Giver of glory,
Helper of souls." Her Judas answered,
Stubborn in mind : "I know not the place
Nor aught of the plain, nor the thing do I know."
Helena spake with angry mind :   685
"This do I swear through the Son of the Maker
The hangèd God, that with hunger thou shalt
Before thy kinsmen be put to death,
Unless thou forsake these lying tales
And plainly to me the truth make known."   690
Then bade she with band him lead alive,
The guilty one cast (the servants delayed not)
Intó a dry pit, where robbed of joy,
He lingered in sorrows seven nights' time
Within the prison oppressed with hunger,   695
Fastened with fetters, and then gan he call,

Weakened by pains, on the seventh day,
Tired and foodless (his strength was exhausted) :
"I you beseech through heaven's God,
That me from these sufferings ye maý release,   700
Humbled by hunger. Of that holy tree
Shall I willingly tell, now longer I may not
For hunger conceal it. This bond is too strong,
Distress too severe, and this misery too hard
In number of days. I maý not endure it,   705
Nor longer conceal of the tree of life,
Though with folly before I was thoroughly filled,
And the truth too late I myself have perceived."

IX.

When she that heard, who men there ordered,
The man's behavior, she quickly commanded   710
That him from confinement and out of his dungeon,
From the narrow abode, they shóuld release.
They hastily thát did soon perform
And him with honor then led they up
From out of the prison as them the queen bade.   715
Stepped they then to the place, the firm-in-mind,
Upon the hill on which the Lord
Before was hanged, heaven-kingdom's Ward,
God's child, on the cross, and yet knew he not well,
Weakened by hunger, where the holy rood   720
Through cunning of foe [1] enclosed in earth,   721-2
Long firm in its bed concealed from men,
Remained in its grave. Now raised he his voice,
Unmindful [2] of might, and in Hebrew he spake :   725

---

[1] No *lacuna* in MS. Gn.[1] inserted one line, but Gn. [2] one word (*fëonda*),
which W. prefers. Text as Z. (*fëondes*), which Sievers approves.
[2] 'Mindful,' Gm. and Gn.; 'suffering,' Z. [?].

"Saviour Lord, thou hast power of rule,
And thou didst create through the might of thy glory
Heaven and earth and the boisterous sea,
The ocean's wide bosom, all creatures alike,
And thou didst measure with thine own hands   730
All the globe of the earth and the heaven above,
And thou thyself sittest, Wielder of victories,
Above the noblest order of angels,
That fly through the air encircled with light,
Great might of glory. There mankind may not   735
From the paths of earth ascend on high
In bodily form with thát bright host,
Heralds of glory. These wroughtest thou,
And for thíne own service thém didst thou set,
Holy and heavenly. Of these in the choir   740
In joy eternal six are named,
Who are surrounded with six wings apiece,
[With them are] adorned, [and] fair they shine.
Of these are four who ever in flight
The service of glory attend upon   745
Before the face of the Judge eternal,
Continually sing in glory the praise,
With clearest voices, of the King of heaven,
Most beauteous of songs, and say these words
With voices pure (their name Cherubím):   750
'Holy is the holy God of archangels,
Ruler of hosts. Full of his glory
Are heaven and earth and all the high powers
With glory distinguished.' There are two among these,
Victor-race in heaven, who Seraphím   755
By name are called. They sháll Paradise
And the tree of life with flaming sword
Holy maintain. The hard-edged trembles,
The etched brand wavers, and changes its form,

Firm in their grips.   Thát,[1] O Lord God,   760
Ever thou wieldest, and thou the sinful,
Guilt-working foes out of the heavens,
The foolish, didst cast.   The accursèd host then
Under dwellings of darkness was forced to fall
To perdition of hell.   There now in the welling   765
Endure they death-pain in the dragon's embrace,
Enclosed in darkness.   [Thee] he resisted,
Thy princely rule; therefore in misery,
Full[2] of all foulness, he guilty shall suffer,
Slavery endure.   There may he not   770
Thy word reject: he is fast in torments,
The author of sin, in misery bound.
If thy will it be, Ruler of angels,
That he may reign who was on the rood,
And who through Mary upon the mid-earth   775
Incarnate became in form of a child,
Prince of the angels (if hé had not been
Thy Son free from sin, never so many
True wonders in world would hé have wrought
In number of days.   Thou wouldst not from death   780
So gloriously him, Ruler of nations,
Have awaked 'fore the hosts, if hé in glory
Through the bright [maid] were not thy Son), —
Now, Father of angels, send forth thy sign.
As thou didst hear the holy man,   785
Moses, in prayer, when thou, God of might,
Didst show to the earl at the noble time
Under the hill-slope the bones of Joseph,
So, Ruler of hosts, if it be thy will,
Through that bright form I'll pray to thee   790
That to me the gold-hoard, Maker of spirits,

---

[1] Referring to the sword.   [2] Gn., or 'foul,' Z.

Thou wilt reveal, that has been from men
[So] long concealed.   Let, Author of life,
Now from this plain a winsome smoke
'Neath heaven's expanse mount up on high   795
Playing in the air.   I'll the better believe,
And I'll the more firmly stablish my mind,
Undoubting trust, upon the hanged Christ,
That hé be in truth the Saviour of souls,
Eternal, Almighty, Israel's King,   800
Forever may have glory in heaven,
Rule without end the dwellings eternal."

X.

Then out of that place a vapor arose
Like smoke 'neath the heavens.   Thére was rejoiced
The mind of the man.   With both his hands,   805
Happy and láw-clever, upward he clapped.
Judas exclaimed, clever in thought :
"Now I in truth myself have known
In my hardened heart that thou art the Saviour
Of [this] mid-earth.   To thee, God of might,   810
Sitting in glory, be thanks without end,
That to me so sad and so full of sin
Thou revealed'st in glory the secrets of fate.
Now, Son of God, to thee will I pray,
Will-giver of peoples, now I know that thou art   815
Declared and born of all kings the Glory,
That thou no longer be of my sins,
Those which I committed by no means seldom,
O Maker, mindful.   Let mé, God of might,
Amid the number of thine own kingdom   820
With the army of saints my dwelling have

In that bright city, where is my brother
Honored in glory, for that faith with thee
He, Stephen, kept, though with handfuls of stones
He was pelted to death. War's meed he has,   825
Fame without end.   There are in books
The wonders he wrought, in writings, made known."
Then gan he glad for the tree of glory,
Constant in zeal, delve in the earth
Beneath the turf, so thát at twenty   830
Feet by measure he found far concealed,
Down in the depths hidden in the earth
'Neath cover of darkness, — there found he three
Of roods together within the sad house
Buried in sand, as in days of old   835
The host of the wicked covered with earth,
The folk of the Jews.   'Gainst the child of God
Hatred they raised, although they should not,
If the lore they'd not heard of the father of lies.
Then wás his mind greatly rejoiced,   840
His heart was strengthened by that holy tree,
His spirit inspired, when the beacon he saw
Holy 'neath earth.   With his hands he clasped
The cross [1] of glory, and it raised 'mid the crowd
From its grave in the earth.   The guests on foot,   845
The æthelings, went on into the city.
They set there in sight three victor-trees
The firm-minded earls 'fore Helena's feet, [2]
Courageous in heart.   The queen rejoiced
In the depth of her soul, and then gan ask   850
On which of those trees the Son of the Ruler,
Joy-giver of heroes, hangèd had been.
" Lo ! thát we have heard through holy books

---

[1] Lit., ' joy-wood.'   [2] Lit., ' knee.'

By tokens declared, that two with him
[Also] suffered, and himself was the third   855
On the tree of the rood.   All heaven was dark
On that terrible day.   Say, if thou canst,
On which of these three the Prince of the angels   ˎ
Suffered [his doom], the Shepherd of glory."
Her Judas might not (he knew not full well)   860
Plainly inform of the victor-wood,
On which one the Saviour uplifted had been,
Victor-son of God, ere he bade them set
Within the middle of that great city
The trees with clamor, and there await   865
Till to him declared the Almighty King
The wonder 'fore the folk of that tree of glory.
The victor-famed sat, their song they raised,
The wise in rede, 'round the three roods
Until the ninth hour; new joy they had   870
With wonder found.   Then came there a crowd,
No little folk, and a man deceased
They brought on a bier with heap of men
In neighborhood [nigh] (ninth hour it was),
A lifeless youth.   Then Judas was there   875
In thought of his heart greatly rejoiced.
He bade then set the soul-less [youth],
Deprived of life the corpse on the earth,
The lifeless one, and up he raised,
Declarer of truth, two of the crosses,   880
The wise, in his arms o'er that fated house,
Plunged deep in thought.   It was dead as before,
Corpse fast on its bier: the limbs were cold,
Clad in distress.   Then was the third
Holy upraised.   The body awaited   885
Until over it the Ætheling's [cross],
His rood, was upraised, Heaven-king's tree,

True token of victory.   Soon he arose
Ready in spirit, both together
Body and soul.   There praise was uplifted   890
Fair 'mid the folk.   The Father they honored,
And also the true Son of the Ruler
They praised in words.   Be glory and thanks
To Him without end from all His creatures.

XI.

Then wás to the people in the depth of their souls   895
Impressed on their minds, as ever shall be,
The wonder that wrought the Lord of hosts
For saving of souls of the race of men,
The Teacher of life.   There the sinner-through-lies
Then stied in the air, the flying fiend.   900
Gan then exclaim the devil of hell,
The terrible monster, mindful of evils :
"Lo ! whát man is this, who now again
With ancient strife my service will ruin,
Increase the old hate, [and] plunder my goods ?   905
This contest's increasing.   The souls cannot,
Workers of sin, longer within
My power remain, now a stranger is come,
Whom I ere reckoned fast in his sins,
Me has he robbed of every right,   910
Of precious possessions.   That's nót a fair course.
To me many harms the Saviour has done,
Contests oppressive, he who in Nazareth
Was reared as a child.   As soon as he grew
From childhood's years, he to hím ever turned   915
Mine own possessions.   I may not now
In any right thrive.   His kingdom is broad

Over the mid-earth.   My might is lessened
Under the heavens.   The rood I need not
Joyfully praise.   Lo! me the Saviour   920
In that narrow home again has confined
Sadly for sorrow.   Through Judas before
Joyful I was, and now am I humbled,
Deprived of goods, through Judas again,
Despised and friendless.   Still can I find   925
Through evil deeds return hereafter [1]
From the homes of the damned.   'Gainst thee will I
      rouse
Another king [2] who will persecute thee,
And he will reject thine own instruction,
And sinful manners of mine will he follow,   930
And thee will he send then into the blackest
And into the worst terrors of torments,
That with sorrow beset thou'lt firmly renounce
The hangèd King whom ere thou obeyed'st."
To him then the cunning Judas replied,   935
The battle-brave man (in him Holy Spirit
Was firmly implanted, fire-hot his love,
His wit was welling with warrior's craft),
And this word he spake with wisdom filled:
"Thou need not so strongly, mindful of sins,   940
Sorrow renew, and strife uprear,
Sin-maker of murder, for thee mighty King
In the depths beneath will thrust thee down,
Worker of sin, to miseries' bottom
Deprived of glory, who many of the dead   945
With his word awaked.   Know thou the readier,
That thou with folly didst once renounce

---

[1] So Z.; 'rebellion for this,' W. See W.'s note.
[2] Julian the Apostate, suggests Gn.

Brightest of lights and love of the Lord,
The fairest joy, and in bath of fire,
Surrounded with torments, didst afterwards dwell,   950
Consumed with flame, and there ever shalt,
Hostile in mind, punishment suffer,
Misery endless." Helena heard
How the fiend and the friend contests aroused,
The blest and the base, on both their sides,   955
The sinner and the saint. Her mind was the gladder
For that she heard the hellish foe
[The fiend] overcome, the worker of sins,
And then she wondered at the wit of the man,
How hé so truthful in so little time   960
And so untaught ever became
With wisdom inspired. [Then] thanked she God,
The King of glory, that her wish was fulfilled
Through the Son of God of each of the two,
Bóth for the sight of the victor-tree,   965
Ánd of the faith that[1] so bright she perceived,
The glorious gift in the breast of the man.

XII.

Thén was made known among that folk,
Throughout that nation widely proclaimed,
The great morning-news for a grievance to many   970
Of those who God's law wished to conceal,
Announced in the towns far as waters embrace,
In each of the cities, that the rood of Christ
Once buried in earth had been discovered,
Brightest of beacons, which since or before   975
Holy 'neath heavens had been upheaved;

---

[1] 'That,' relative, though it may be taken as conjunction, as Z.

And it was to the Jews the greatest of sorrows,
Unhappy men, most hateful of fates,
That they 'fore the world were unable to change it,
The joy of the Christians.   Then bade the queen   980
'Mong the host of earls heralds to hasten,
Quickly to journey; they should of the Romans
O'er the high sea the lord seek out,
And to that warrior the best of tidings
Say, to himself, that the victor-sign   985
Through Creator's favor had been recovered,
Found in the earth, which ages before
Had been concealed for sorrow to saints,
To Christian folk.   Then was to the king
Through the glorious words his spirit gladdened,   990
His heart rejoicing.   Then was of inquirers
'Neath golden garments no lack in the cities
Come from afar.   To him greatest of comforts
It became in the world at the wished-for tidings, —
His heart delighted, — which army-leaders   995
Over the east-ways, messengers, brought him,
How happy a journey over the swan-road
The men with the queen successfully made
To the land of the Greeks.   The Cæsar bade them
With greatest haste again prepare   1000
Themselves for the way.   The men delayed not
As soon as they had the answer heard,
The words of the ætheling.   Bade he Helena hail,
The war-famed greet, if they the sea-voyage
And happy journey were able to make,   1005
Brave-minded men, to the holy city.
Bade also to her the messengers say
Constantínus, that she a church
On the mountain-slope for gain of both
Should there erect, a temple of God,   1010

On Calvarý, for joy to Christ,
For help to men, where the holy rood
Had béen discovered, greatest of trees,
Of those that earth-dwellers ever heard named
Upon the earth. So she effected,   1015
After dear kinsmen brought from the west
Over the ocean many loved tidings.
Then bade the queen those skilled in crafts
To seek out apart, the best of all,
Those who most cunningly knew how to work   1020
In joinings of stones, on the open plain
God's temple to build. As the Warden of spirits
Her counselled from heaven, she bade the rood
With gold adorn and gems of all kinds,
With the most splendid of precious stones   1025
To set with skill, and in silver chest
To enclose with locks. There that tree of life,
Best of victor-trees, has since remained
In nature eternal.[1] There 'twill be ever ready
A help to the sick 'gainst every ill,   1030
Distress and sorrow. There soon will they
Through that holy creation assistance obtain,
A gift divine. Also Judas received
After fixed time the bath of baptism,
And cleansed became, trustful in Christ,   1035
Dear to the Life-warden. His faith became
Firm in his heart, when the Spirit of comfort
Made his abode in the breast of the man,
To repentance him urged. The better he chose,
The joy of glory, and the worse he refused,   1040
The service of idols, and error rejected,
Unlawful belief. To him King[2] eternal,
The Creator, was mild, God, Ruler of might.

---

[1] So Z.; 'The noble wood,' Gm. and Gn.   [2] Latin, *rex*.

XIII.

Then hé was baptized who often before
The ready light [had long rejected, Gh.], 1045
Inspired was his soul for that better life,
To glory turned. Fate surely ordained
That so full of faith and so dear to God
In realm of the world he should become,
[So] pleasing to Christ. That known became, 1050
After that Helena bade them Eusebius,
Bishop of Rome, into council with her
To bring for help, the very wise [man]
By means of men,[1] to the holy city, ·
That he might ordain to the sacred office 1055
Judas for the folk in Jerúsalém,
To be their bishop within the city,
Through gift of the Spirit for the temple of God
Chosen with wisdom, and him Cyriácus
Through counsel of wit she afterwards named 1060
A second time.´ The name was changed
Of the man in the city henceforth for the better,
For the law of the Saviour. Then still Helena's
Mind was disturbed at the wondrous fate,
Very much for the nails, those which the Saviour's 1065
Feet had pierced through and likewise his hands,
With which on the rood the Ruler of Heaven,
Lord mighty, was fastened. Of these gan ask
The Christians' queen, Cyriacus prayed
That still for her, by the might of his spirit, 1070
For the wondrous fate the will he 'ld fulfil,
Reveal by his gifts, and shé addressed
This word to the bishop, boldly she spake :

---

[1] So Z.; ' With pomp of array,' Gn.

"'Thou, earls' defence, the noble tree
Of heavens' King me rightly didst show,   1075
On which was hanged by heathen hands
The Helper of spirits, own Son of God,
Saviour of men.   Still of the nails
In thought of my mind curiosity troubles me.
I would thou should'st find those which yet in the
     earth   1080
Deeply buried remain concealed,
Hidden in darkness.   My heart ever sorrows,
Sad it complains and never will rest,
Ere for mé He fulfil, Almighty Father,
Ruler of hosts, mine own desire,   1085
Saviour of men, by sight[1] of the nails,
The Holy from height.   Now quickly do thou
With all humility, most excellent man,
Direct thy prayer to the heavens bright,
To the Ruler of glory, pray Strength of warriors,   1090
That to thee may reveal the Almighty King
The hord 'neath the earth, that hidden still,
Concealed from men, in secret abides."
Then gan the holy one strengthen his heart,
Inspired in his breast the bishop of the folk,   1095
Glad-minded, went with a crowd of men
Those praising God, and earnestly then
Cyriacús on Calvarý
Inclined his face, his secret concealed not,
With might of his spirit called upon God   1100
With all humility, prayed Warden of angels
To open to him the únknown fate
In his new distress, where he the nails
Upon the plain best need expect.

---

[1] Lit., 'coming.'

Then caused he the token, where they were looking,   1105
The Father, hope's Spirit, in form of fire
Upwards to rise, where they most noble
By means of men[1] had once been hidden
With secret cunning, the nails in the earth.
Then suddenly came brighter than sun   1110
The playing flame.   The people saw
To the giver of their will[2] the wonder made known,
When there out of darkness, like stars of heaven
Or gems of gold, upon the bottom
The nails from the narrow bed shining beneath   1115
Brilliantly glittered.   The people rejoiced,
The glad-minded host, spake glory to God
With one accord all, though ere they were
By the devil's deceit long in error,
Estranged from Christ.   Thus did they speak: 1120
"Ourselves now we see the token of victory,
True wonder of God, that before we opposed
With lying words.   Now is come into light,
Is revealed, fate's course.   May glory for this
Have in the highest heaven-kingdom's God!"   1125
Then he was rejoiced who turned to repentance
Through the Son of God, the people's bishop,
A second time.   He took the nails,
Disturbed with fear, and to the venerable
Queen did he bring them.   Cyriacus had   1130
It all fulfilled as the noble one bade him,
The woman's will.   There was sound of weeping,
Hot head-welling was poured o'er her cheeks,
By no means for sorrow.   The tears were falling
O'er the plaiting of wires.[3]   With glory fulfilled   1135

---

[1] Same expression as in 1054.   [2] Lit., 'will-giver,' *i.e.*, the queen.
[3] *i.e.*, her ornaments of gold.

Was the wish of the queen.   She knelt on her knees
With bright belief; she honored the gift,
Rejoicing with joy, which wás to her brought
For help in her sorrows.   Then thanked she God,
The Lord of victories, that the truth she had learnt   1140
At that present time, that oft was announced
So long before from creation of the world
For comfort to the people.   Shé was inspired
With the gift of wisdom, and his dwelling held
Holy Spirit of heaven, guarded her breast,   1145
Her noble heart.   So her the Almighty
Victor-son of God after protected.

XIV.

Then eagerly gan she with secrets of soul
Seek in her spirit by soothfastnéss
The way to glory.   Now God of hosts   1150
His help bestowed, the Father in heaven,
Almighty King, that the queen obtained
Her will in the world.   The prophecy was
By sages of old sung long before
All from beginning, as it afterwards happened   1155
In respect to each thing.   The folk-queen began
Through gift of the Spirit gladly to seek
With greatest care how best the nails,
And in manner most worthy, she might apply
For joy to the folk, what was will of the Lord.   1160
Bade she then fetch a very wise man
Quickly to counsel, him who wisdom
Through clever might thoroughly knew,
Wise in his heart, and gan him ask
What in his soul seemed to him best   1165
To do about that, and his teachings she chose

In respect to her conduct.   Her boldly [1] he answered :
"That is becoming that word of the Lord
Thou hold in heart, holy counsel,
Most excellent queen, and the King's command   1170
Gladly fulfil, now God has thee given
Success of soul and craft of wit,
The Saviour of men.   Bid thou these nails
For that most excellent of earthly kings,
Of owners of cities, put on his bridle   1175
For bit to his horse.   To many that shall,
Throughout the mid-earth, become renowned,
When with that in contest he may overcome
Each one of his foes, when the brave-in-war
On either side the battle seek,   1180
Sword-contenders, where they strive for victory,
Foe against foe.   War-speed shall he have,
Victory in fight and everywhere peace,
In battle success, who carries in front
The bridle on horse, when the famed-in-fight   1185
At clashing of spears, the choicest of men,
Bear shield and lance.   To each one of men
Against war-terror shall be invincible
This weapon in war.   The seer of it sang,
Cunning in thought.   Deep moved his mind,   1190
His wit of wisdom.   This word he spake :
'That shall be known that the horse of the king
Shall 'neath the proud with bit be adorned,
With bridle-rings.   That beacon to God
Shall holy be called, and that one valor-blessed,   1195
Honored in war, who rides on that horse.'"
With haste then that did all perform
Helena 'fore earls, bade the ætheling's,

---

[1] Gn.'s emendation.

Heroes' ring-giver's, bridle adorn,
To her own son sent as a present   1200
O'er ocean's stream the blameless gift.
She bade then together those whom as best
Of men she knew among the Jews,
Of the race of heroes, to the holy city,
To the town to come.   Then gan the queen   1205
The dear ones teach that love of the Lord
And peace likewise among themselves,
The bond of friendship, they fast should hold
Without reproach in time of their life,
And they to the teacher's lore should hearken,   1210
The Christian virtues that Cyriacus taught them,
Clever in books.   The office of bishop
Was fairly made fast.   From afar oft to him
The lame, the sick, the crippled came,
The halt, the wounded, the leprous and blind,   1215
The lowly, the sad ; always there health
At the hands of the bishop, healing, they found
Ever for ever.   Yet Helena gave him
Treasures as presents, when ready she was
For the journey home, and bade she then all   1220
In that kingdom of men who worshipped God,
Men and women, that they should honor
With mind and might that famous day,
With thoughts of the heart, whereon holy rood
Had béen discovered, greatest of trees,   1225
Of those which from earth ever sprang up
Grown under leaves.   Then spring was gone
Except six nights ere coming of summer
On the kalends of May.   To each of those men
Be hell's door shut, heaven's unclosed,   1230
Eternally opened the kingdom of angels,
Joy without end, and their portion appointed

Along with Mary, who takes into mind
That one most dear of festal days
Of that rood under heaven, that which the mightiest   1235
Ruler of all with arm protected.   *Finit.*[1]

XV.

Thus old and death-ready in this frail house
Word-craft I wove and wondrously framed it,
Reflected at times and sifted my thought-
Closely at night. I knew not well   1240
The truth of the rood,[2] ere wider knowledge
Through glorious might into thought of my mind
Wisdom revealed to me. I was stained with crimes,
Fettered with sins, pained with sorrows,
Bitterly bound, banefully vexed,   1245
Ere lore to me lent through light-bringing office
For help to the agèd, his blameless gift
The mighty King meted, and poured in my mind,
Brightness disclosed, widened with time,
Bone-house unbound, breast-lock unwound,   1250
Song-craft unlocked, which I joyfully used,
With will, in the world. Of that tree of glory
Often not once meditation I had,
Ere that wonder I had revealed
About that bright tree, as in books I found   1255
In course of events, in writings declared
Of that beacon of victory. Ay till then was the man
With care-waves oppressed, a flickering *pine-torch* [c],
Though he in the mead-hall treasures received,
Apples of gold.[3] Mourned for his *bow* [y]   1260

---

[1] Here properly ends the legend of the Finding of the Cross. The last
canto contains reflections of the poet.
[2] Gn.'s emendation.   [3] Lit., 'appled gold.'

The comrade of *sorrow* [N], suffered distress,
His secret constrained, where before him the *horse* [E]
Measured the mile-paths, with spirit ran
Proud of his ornaments.   *Hope* [W] is decreased,
Joy, after years, youth is departed,   1265
The ancient pride.   The *bison* [U] was once
The gladness of youth.   Now are the old days
In course of time gone forever,
Life-joy departed, as *ocean* [L] flows by,
Waves hurried along.   To each one is *wealth*[1] [F]   1270
Fleeting 'neath heaven, treasures of earth
Pass 'neath the clouds likest to wind,
When before men it mounts up aloud,
Roams 'round the clouds, raging rushes,
And then all at once silent becomes,   1275
In narrow prison closely confined,
Strongly repressed.   So passes this world,
And likewise besides what things[2] have been
In it produced flame will consume,
When the Lord himself judgment will seek   1280
With host of angels.   Every one there
Of speech-bearing men the truth shall hear
Of every deed through mouth of the Judge,
And likewise of words the penalty pay
Of all that with folly were spoken before,   1285
Of daring thoughts.   Then parts into three
Into clutch of fire each one of folk,
Of those that have dwelt in course of time
Upon the broad earth.   The righteous shall be
Upmost in flame, host of the blessed,   1290
Crowd eager for glory, as they may bear it,

---

[1] The words in italics are the names of the runes that make up the name CYNEWULF. This artificial use of words makes the interpretation obscure, and scholars differ about it.   [2] Or, 'those who.'

And without torment easily suffer,
Band of the brave. For them shall be moderate
The brightness of flame,[1] as it shall be easiest,
Softest for them. The sinful shall be,   1295
Those spotted with evil, compressed in the middle,
Men sad-in-mind, within the hot waves
Smothered with smoke. The third part shall be,
Accursèd sinners, in the flood's abyss,
False folk-haters, fastened in flame   1300
For deeds of old, gang of the godless
In grip of the gledes. To God never more
From that place of torment come they in mind,
To the King of glory, but théy shall be cast
From that terrible fire to the bottom of hell,   1305
The workers of woe. To the [other] two parts
It will be unlike. They may angels' Lord,
Victories' God, see. Théy shall be cleansed,
Sundered from sins, as smelted gold,
That is in the flame from every spot   1310
Through fire of the oven thoroughly cleansed,
Freed and refined. So shall each of those men
Be freed and made pure from every sin,
From heavy crimes through fire of that doom.
Then afterwards théy may peace enjoy,   1315
Eternal bliss. To them angels' Warden
Shall be mild and gentle, for that théy every evil
Despised, sins' work, and to Son of their Maker
They called with words. Hence in beauty they
    shine now .
Like to the angels, the heritage have   1320
Of the King of glory for ever and ever. Amen.

---

[1] Gn., Z.

JUDITH.

IX.

*   *   *   *   *   *   *   *

[The glorious Creator's][1] gifts doubted she [not]
Upón this wide earth; then found she there ready
Help from the mighty Prince, when she most need
    did have
Of grace from the highest Judge, that her 'gainst
    the greatest terror
The Lord of Creation should shield. That Father
    in heaven to her
The Glorious-in-mind did grant, for thát firm faith
    she had
Ín the Almighty ever. Then heard I that Holofernes
Wine-summons eagerly wrought, and wíth all won-
    ders a glorious
Banquet had hé prepared; to thát bade the prince
    of men
All his noblest thanes. Thát with mickle haste   10
Did the warriors-with-shields perform; came to the
    mighty chief
The people's leaders going. Ón the fourth day was
    that
After that Judith, cunning in mind,
The elf-sheen virgin, him first had sought.

---

[1] Gn.'s emendation to fill *lacuna* of MS.

X.

They then at the feast proceeded to sit,   15
The proud to the wine-drinking, all his comrades-
    in-ill,
Bold mailèd-warriors. There were lofty beakers
Oft borne along the benches, alsó were cups and
    flagons
Full to the hall-sitters borne. The fated partook of
    them,
Brave warriors - with - shields, though the mighty
    weened not of ít,   20
Awful lord of earls. Thén was Holofernes,
Gold-friend of men, full of wine-joy:
He laughed and clamored, shouted and dinned,
That children of men from afar might hear
How the strong-minded both stormed and yelled,   25
Moody and mead-drunken, often admonished
The sitters-on-benches to bear themselves [1] well.
Thus did the hateful one during all day
His liege-men [loyal] keep plying with wine,
Stout-hearted giver of treasure, untíl they lay in a
    swoon,   30
He drenched all his nobles [with drink], as if they
    were slain in death,
Deprived [2] of each one of goods. Thus bade the
    prince of men
The sitters-in-hall to serve, untíl to children of men
The darkening night drew nigh. He bade then,
    filled with hate,
The blessed maiden with haste to fetch   35
To his bed of rest, laden with jewels,

---

[1] 'Loudly carouse,' Kr. and C.   [2] 'Gorged with,' Kr. and C.

Adorned with rings.   They quickly performed,
The attendant thanes, what their lord them bade,
Mailed-warriors' prince; like a flash they stepped
Into the guest-room, where they Judith   40
Wise-minded found, and quickly then
The warriors-with-shields began to lead
The glorious maid to the lofty tent
Where the mighty himself always[1] rested
By night within, to the Saviour hateful,   45
Holofernes.   There wás an all-golden
Beautiful fly-net around the folk-warrior's
Bed suspended, só that the hateful
Was able to look through, the chief of warriors,
Upon each one that therein came   50
Of the sons of heroes, and on him no one
Of the race of men, unless the proud some one
Of the strong-in-war bade to him nearer
Of warriors for counsel to come.   They then to him
  at rest brought
Quickly the cunning woman; went then the stout-
  in-heart   55
The men their lord to tell that the holy woman was
Brought to his chamber-tent.   The famous then in
  mind
Was glad, the ruler of cities; he thought the beauti-
  ful maiden
With spot and stain to defile: that Judge of glory
  would not
Allow, the Keeper of honor, but him from that deed
  restrained   60
The Lord, the Ruler of hosts.   Went then the devil-
  ish one,

---

1 Or, 'after feast.'

The wanton [warrior-prince],[1] with [mickle] band of
    men,
The baleful his bed to seek, where hé his life should
    lose
Quickly within one night; he had then his end at-
    tained [2]
On earth ungentle [end], such as before he wrought
    for,   65
The mighty prince of men, while ín this world he was,
While he dwèlt under roof of the clouds.   Then fell
    so drunk with wine
The mighty [chief]. on his bed, as if he knew no rede
Within his place of wit; the warriors stepped   ·
Oút from the chamber with mickle haste,   70
The wine-filled men, whó the oath-breaker,
Hateful folk-hater, had led to his bed
For the very last time.   Then was the Saviour's
Glorious maiden earnestly mindful
How she the terrible most easily might   75
Of life deprive before the lustful,
The wanton, awoke.   The wreathed-locked took then,
The Creator's handmaid, a sharp-edged sword
Hardened by war-strokes [?],[3] and drew from its
    sheath   ,
With hér right hand; then Keeper of heaven   80
By name she gan name, Saviour of all
Dwellers-in-th' world, and this word she spake:
"Thee, God of Creation, and Spirit of Comfort,
Son of the Almighty, will I [now] pray
For thine own mercy to me in my need,   85
Trinity's Glory.   To me greatly now then

---

[1] 'King,' Gn. and Kr., but *gúðfreca* suits the verse better than *cyning*,
and even that is not metrically sufficient to fill the *lacuna*.
    [2] Lit., 'awaited.'   [3] So Gn.?   'Scouring,' Sw.?, Kr.?, C,

My heart is inflamed, and my mind is sad,
Sorely with sorrows oppressed; grant, Lord of Heaven,
    to me
Victory and faith without fear, that I with this sword
    may be able
To hew down this dealer of murder; grant [too] my
    safety to me,   90
Strong-hearted Leader of men; ne'er in this world
    had I
Of thy mercy more urgent need: avenge now, mighty
    Lord,
Glorious Giver of honor, that I am so angry in mind,
So heated within my breast." Hér then the highest
    Judge
Quickly with courage inspired, as doth he [ever]
    each one   95
Of dwellers here [upon earth], who him for help to
    them seek
With rede and righteous belief. · Then roomy in
    mind she became,
The holy one's hope was renewed; then took she the
    heathen man
Fast by his own [long] hair, with hands him towards
    her she drew
With marks of contempt, and the baleful one   100
With cunning laid down, the loathsome man,
As she the accursèd most easily might
Wield at her will. Struck then the curly-locked
The hostile foe with shining [1] sword,
The hateful-minded, that half-way she cut   105
The [evil one's] neck, that he lay in a swoon,
Drunken and wounded. Not yet was he dead,

---

[1] 'Hostile,' Sw.?

Thoroughly lifeless; struck she then earnestly,
The maiden brave-minded, a second time
The heathen hound, that his head rolled off   110
Forth on the floor: the foul corpse lay
Lifeless behind, went the spirit elsewhere
Beneath the deep earth, and there was disgraced,
In torment bound ever thereafter,
Surrounded with serpents, with tortures encompassed,   115
Strongly enchained in the fire of hell
After his death.   He need never hope,
Enveloped with darkness, that thence he may go
Out of that worm-hall, but there shall he dwell
Ever for ever without end henceforth   120 .
In thát dark home, of hope-joys deprived.

XI.

Then had she gained glorious honor,
Judith in war, as God to her granted,
The Ruler of Heaven, who gave to her victory.
The cunning maid then quickly brought   125
The army-leader's head so bloody
In that [very] vessel in which her attendant,
The fair-faced woman, food for them both,
In virtues renowned, thither had brought,
And it then so gory to her gave in hand,   130
To the thoughtful-in-mind to bear to their home,
Judith to her maid.   Went they forth thence,
The women both in courage bold,
Until they had come, proud in their minds,
The women triumphant, out from the army,   135
Só that they plainly were able to see
Of that beautiful city the walls [fair] shine,

Béthulía.   Then jewel-decked théy
Upon the foot-path hastened to go,
Until glad-minded they had arrived   140
At the gate of the wall.   The warriors sat,
The watching men, were keeping ward
Within that fortress, as before to the folk,
Sad in their minds, Judith had bidden,
The cunning maiden, when she went on her journey,   145
The stout-hearted woman.   Then again was she come,
Dear to her people, and then quickly ordered
The wise-minded woman some one of the men
To come to meet her from out the wide city,
And hér in haste to admit within   150
Through the gate of the wall, and this word she spake
To the victor-folk: "To you can I say
A thought-worthy [1] thing, that no longer ye need
Mourn in your minds: your Creator is kind,
Glory of kings: that ís become known   155
Wide through the world, that to you is success
Glorious at hand, and honor is granted
For [all] those sorrows which long ye suffered."
Glad then were they, the dwellers-in-borough,
After they heard how the holy one spake   160
O'er the high wall.—The host was in joy.
To the fortress-gate the people hastened,
Men, women together, in troops and heaps,
In crowds and throngs, hurried and ran
To meet the Lord's maid by thousands and thou-
          sands,   165
Both old and young: to eàch one became
Of men in the mead-city his mind rejoiced,
After they knew that Judith was come   .

---

[1] 'Thank-worthy,' Kr.

Again to her home, and then in haste
With reverence théy allowed her to enter.   170
Then bade the clever, with gold adorned,
Her servant-maid, thoughtful-in-mind,
The army-leader's head to uncover,
And ít as a proof bloody to show
To the city-folk how she speeded in war.   175
Then spake the noble one to all the folk :
"Here ye may clearly, victory-blessed warriors,
Chiefs of the people, upón the most hateful
Heathen hero's head fix your gaze,
On Holofernes deprived of life,   180
Who chiefest of men wrought murders for us,
Sorest sorrows, and that yet more
Would he increase : but God him granted not
A longer life, that hé with woes
Might still afflict us.   Of life I deprived him   185
By help of God.   Now I every man
Of these city-dwellers will [earnestly] pray,
Of shield-bearing warriors, that ye yourselves quickly
Hasten to fight; when the God of creation,
The glorious King, shall send from the east   190
Bright beams of light, bear forth your shields,
Boards before breasts and coats-of-mail,
Bright helmets [too] among the foes,
To fell the folk-leaders with shining swords,
The fated chiefs.   Your foes are now   195
Condemned to death, and ye glory shall gain,
Honor in battle, as to you hath betokened
The mighty Lord through mine own hand."
Then the band of the brave was quickly prepared,
Of the bold for battle; stepped out the valiant   200
Men and comrades, bore their banners,
Went forth to fight straight on their way

The heroes 'neath helmets from the holy city
At the dawn itself; shields made a din,
Loudly resounded. Thereat laughed the lank   205
Wolf in the wood, and the raven wan,
Fowl greedy for slaughter: both of them knew
That for them the warriors thought to provide
Their fill on the fated; and flew on their track
The dewy-winged eagle eager for prey,   210
The dusky-coated sang his war-song,
The crooked-beaked. Stepped forth the warriors,
The heroes for battle with boards protected,
With hollow shields, who awhile before
The foreign-folk's reproach endured,   215
The heathens' scorn; fiercely was thát
At the ash-spear's play to them all repaid,
[All] the Assyrians, after the Hebrews
Under their banners had [boldly] advanced
To the army-camps. They bravely then   220
Forthright let fly showers of arrows,
Of battle-adders, óut from the horn-bows,
Of strongly-made shafts; stormed they aloud,
The cruel warriors, sent forth their spears
Among the brave; the heroes were angry,   225
The dwellers-in-land, with the loathéd race;
The stern-minded stepped, the stout-in-heart,
Rudely awakened their ancient foes
Weary from mead; with hands drew forth
The men from the sheaths the brightly-marked swords   230
Most choice in their edges, eagerly struck
Of the [host of] Assyrians the battle-warriors,
The hostile-minded; not one they spared
Of the army-folk, nor low nor high
Of living men, whom théy might subdue.   235

XII.

Thus then the thanes in the morning-hours
Pressed on the strangers unceasinglý,
Until they perceived, those who were hostile,
The army-folk's chiefest leaders,.
That upón them sword-strokes mighty bestowed   240
The Hebrew men.   They thát in words
To their most noted chiefs of the people
Went to announce, waked helmeted warriors
And to thém with fear the dread news told,
To the weary-from-mead the morning-terror,   245
The hateful sword-play. ⌐ Then learnt I that quickly
The slaughter-fated men aroused from sleep
Ánd to the baleful's sleeping-bower
The saddened [1] men pressed ón in crowds,
To Holofernes : they only were thinking   250
To their own lord to make known the fight,
Ere terror on him should take its seat,
The might of the Hebrews.   They all imagined
That the prince of men and the handsome maid
In the beautiful tent were [still] together,   255
Judith the noble and the lustful one,
Dreadful and fierce; though no earl there was
Whó the warrior durst [then] awake,
Or durst discover how the helmeted warrior
With the holy maid had passed his time,   260
The Creator's handmaid.   The force approached,
The folk of the Hebrews, courageously fought
With hard battle-arms, fiercely repaid
Their former fights with shining [2] swords,

---

[1] So Sw.; ' weary in mind,' Gn., Kr., C.
[2] ' Hostile,' C., though ' flashing,' 194, ' and gleaming,' 302.

The old-time grudge; was óf the Assyrians   265
By thát day's work the glory diminished,
The pride brought low.   The warriors stood   .
'Round their prince's tent strongly excited,
Gloomy in mind.   They then all together
Began to groan,[1] to cry aloud   270
And gnash with their teeth, — afar from God, —
Showing their anger; 'twas the end of their glory,
Of joy and valor.   The earls were thinking
To awaken their lord; they did not succeed.
Then at last and too late was one so bold   275
Of the battle-warriors that to the bower-tent
He daringly ventured, since need him compelled:
Found he then on the bed lying deadly-pale
His [own] gold-giver of breath bereft,
Of life deprived.   Then quickly he fell   280
Astounded to earth, gan tear his hair,
Excited in mind, and his garments too,
And this word he spake to the warriors [brave],
Who saddened there were standing without:
"Here is displayed our own destruction,   285
The future betokened, that it is to the time
Now amongst men[2] almost arrived,   .
When wé our lives shall lose together,
In battle perish: here lies with sword hewn
Our lord beheaded."   They then sad-in-mind   290
Threw down their weapons and sorrowful went
To hasten in flight.   They fought on their tracks,
The mighty folk, till the greatest part
Of the army lay, in battle struck down,
On the victor-plain, hewn down with swords,   295

---

[1] Lit., 'cough.'
[2] So Gn. and Kr.; 'with violence,' Sw.; 'with afflictions,' C.

To wolves for pleasure, and to slaughter-greedy
Fowls for a joy. Those who lived fled
The shields of their foes.[1] Went on their tracks
The Hebrews' host, honored with victory,
With glory ennobled; them took the Lord God   300
Fairly to help, the Lord Almighty.
They bravely then with shining swords,
Stout-hearted heroes, a war-path wrought
Through heaps of their foes, hewed down their shields,
Cut through their phalanx: the warriors were   305
Enraged in battle, the Hebrew men;
The thanes at that time were much delighted
At the combat with spears. Here fell in the dust
The highest part of the chiefest number
Óf the Assyrians' princely nobility,   310
Of the hateful race; very few came
Alive to their homes. The nobly-bold turned,
Warriors retiring, among the slaughtered,
The smoking corpses; it was time to take
For the dwellers-in-land from the loathsome ones,   315
Their ancient foes deprived of life,
The gory booty, the shining trappings,
Shields and broad swords, brown-colored helmets,
Precious treasures. Gloriously had they
On thát folk-place their foes overcome,   320
The defenders of home their ancient foes
With swords put-to-sleep: behind them rested
Those who in life were most hateful to them
Of living races. Then all the people,
Of tribes most renowned, for one month's space,   325
The proud twisted-locked, bore and carried
To that bright city, Bethulia [named],

---

[1] So Sw. and Kr.; 'Of the hostile shield-warriors,' Gn. and C.

Helmets and hip-swords, hoary byrnies,
War-trappings of men adorned with gold,
More precious treasures than any man   330
Of the cunning-in-mind may be able to tell,
All that the warriors with might had won,
The bold under banners on the battle-place
By means of Judith's [most] clever lore,
The moody[1] maid's.   As meed for her   335
From that expedition, they brought for herself,
The spear-strong earls, of Holofernes
The sword and gory helm, likewise the byrnie broad,
Adorned with reddish gold, all that the warrior-chief,
The brave, of treasure had, or individual wealth,   340
Of rings and jewels bright; thát to the lady fair,
The wise-in-mind, gave théy.   For all that Judith said.
Glory to the Lord of hosts, who honor to her gave,
Fame in realm of earth, and meed in heaven too,
Reward in the glory of heaven, because true faith
        she had   345
In.the Almighty ever; now at last she doubted not
Of the meed which long she yearned for.   For that
        to the dear Lord be
Glory for ever and ever, who made both wind and air,
The heavens and roomy lands, likewise the rushing
        streams,
And joys of firmament too by means of his mercy
        mild.   350

---

[1] *i.e.*, 'spirited.'

ATHELSTAN,

OR

THE FIGHT AT BRUNANBURH.

—◦◦—

ÆTHELSTAN King, of earls the lord,
Of heroes ring-giver, and his brother too,
Edmund Ætheling, enduring fame
Earned in the fight with edges of swords
By Brunanburh. The board-wall they cleaved,   5
The war-shields hewed with leavings of hammers
The sons of Edward. 'Twas natural to them
By right of descent that in battle they oft
'Gainst every foe their land defended,
Their hoards and homes. The foes were fallen,   10
Folk of the Scots and men of the ships,
Fated they fell. The field ran thick [1]
With heroes' blood, when the risen sun
At morning-time, the mighty orb,
Shone o'er the earth, bright candle of God,   15
Eternal Lord, till the noble creature
Sank to his rest. There many men lay
Struck down [2] with spears, men from the North,
Shot o'er the shield, and Scotsmen too,
Weary [and] war-filled. The West-Saxons forth   20
The live-long day with legions of warriors

---

[1] Lit., 'became slippery,' Gn.; 'babbled' (as a brook), or 'became dark,' Kr.; 'streamed,' Th.   [2] 'Scattered,' Th.

Pressed on the heels of the hostile foes;
They felled the fleers with force from behind
With sharp-ground swords.   Shrank not the Mercians
From hard hand-play with any of heroes,   25
Of those who with Anlaf o'er welling of waves
On the deck of the ship had sought the land,
Fated for fight.   Five of them lay
On the battle-field, young kings [they were],
Slaughtered[1] with swords, and also seven   30
Earls of Anlaf, and unnumbered host
Of seamen and Scots.   There was forced to flee
The Northmen's chief, by need compelled
To the prow of his ship with few attendants.
Keel crowded[2] the sea, the king went forth   35
On the fallow flood; he saved his life.
There too the agèd escaped by flight
To his home in the North, Constantínus.
The hoar war-hero was unable to boast
Of attendance of men; he was robbed of his kinsmen,   40
Bereaved of his friends on the battle-field,
Conquered in fight, and he left his son
On the place of slaughter wasted with wounds,
The boy in the battle.   He durst not boast,
The gray-haired warrior, of the clash of swords,   45
The agèd enemy, nor Anlaf the more.
With their army-remnant they durst not rejoice
That in deeds of war they proved to be better
On the place of battle, the striking of standards,
The mingling of spears, the meeting of men,   50
The clashing of weapons, when on slaughter-field
In contest with Edward's sons they contended.

---

[1] Lit., 'put to sleep.'
[2] Or, 'He pressed ship on the sea'; 'drove,' Th.

Departed the Northmen in nailèd ships,
Drear remnant of darts, on the sea of Dyng[1] [?],
O'er the water deep Dublin to seek,   55
Back to land of the Erse, depressed in mind.
Likewise the brothers both together,
King and ætheling, were seeking their home,
West-Saxons' land, exulting in war.
Behind them they let the corpses share   60
The dark-feathered fowl, the raven black,
The crooked-beaked, and the ashy-feathered,
White-tailed eagle enjoy the prey,
The greedy war-hawk, and the gray-clad beast,
The wolf in the wood.   More corpses there wére not   65
Upon this island ever as yet
Of folk down-felled before this time
With edges of sword, as books to us tell,
Sages of old, since hither from East
Angles and Saxons came to this land,   70
O'er the broad ocean Britain [once] sought,
Haughty war-smiths the Welsh overcame,
Earls eager for honor this earth acquired.

---

[1] Gn. and W. take *Dyng* as a proper name, but no one knows who
Dyng was. Kr. leaves *on dynges mere* untranslated, with the remark:
"*ist unaufgeklärt.*" He thinks it refers to some bay in Ireland, from which
the invaders set out, but why may it not be a name for the Irish Sea itself?
Th. translates ' on the roaring sea,' but adds ' quite conjectural.'

BYRHTNOTH,

OR

THE FIGHT AT MALDON.

———○◇○———

*　*　*　*　*　* was broken.
Then bade he each youth his horse to forsake,
To hasten afar and forwards to go,
Be mindful of might, of mood courageous.
This Offa's kinsman at once perceived   5
That the earl was unwilling faint heart to endure.
Then he let from his hands his lief [1] hawk fly,
His hawk to the holt, and to battle he stepped;
By thát might one know that the knight was un-
　　willing
To be weak in the war when to weapons he took.   10
By him too would Eadric, by his overlord, stand,
His chief in the fight; then forth gan he bear
His spear to the battle: brave spirit had he
The while that with hands he was able to hold
Shield and broad sword; his boast he fulfilled,[2]   15
When hé 'fore his lord was bound to fight.
There Byrhtnoth gan then his warriors embolden,
Rode and gave rede, instructed his men
Hów they should stand, and the stead sustain,
And bade that rimmed shields they rightly should
　　hold   20

---

[1] Dear.　　　　　　　　[2] Or, 'maintained.'

Fast with their fists, and frightened be never.
When hé had the folk fairly emboldened,
With his men he alighted where was liefest to him,
Whére his hearth-followers most faithful he knew.
Then stood on the stathe,[1] stoutly did call　　25
The wikings' herald, with words he spake,
Who boastfully bore fróm the brine-farers·
An errand to th' earl, where he stood on the shore:
"To thee me did send the seamen snell,[2]
Bade to thee say, thou must send to them quickly　　30
Bracelets for safety; and 'tis better for you
That *ye* this spear-rush with tribute buy off
Than *we* in so fierce a fight engage.
We need not each spill,[3] if ye speed to this:
We will for the pay a peace confirm.　　35
If thou that redest who art highest in rank,
If thou thy lieges art willing to loose,
To pay to the seamen at their own pleasure
Money for peace, and take peace from us,
We will with the treasure betake us to ship,　　40
Fare on the flood, and peace with you confirm."
Byrhtnoth replied, his buckler uplifted,
Waved his slim spear, with words he spake,
Angry and firm gave answer to him:
"Hear'st thou, seafarer, what saith this folk?　　45
They will for tribute spear-shafts you pay,
Poisonous points and trusty[4] swords,
Those weapons that you in battle avail not.
Herald of seamen, hark[5] back again,
Say to thy people much sadder words,　　50
Here stands not unknown an earl with his band,
Whó will defend this father-land,

---

[1] Bank.　　[2] Bold.　　[3] Destroy.　　[4] Lit., 'old.'　　[5] Lit., 'announce.'

Æthelred's home, mine own liege lord's,
His folk and field: ye 're fated to fall,
Ye heathen, in battle. (Too base it me seems   55
That ye with our scats [1] to ship may go
Unfought against, so far ye now hither
Intó our country have come within;
Ye shall not so gently treasure obtain;
Shall spear and sword sooner beseem us,   60
Grim battle-play, ere tribute we give."
Then bade he shield bear, warriors advance,
So that on the burn-stathe [2] they all were standing.
Might not thére for the water one war-band to th' other,
When flowing flood came after the ebb,   65
Sea-streams interlocked; too long seemed it them
Till they together their spears should bear.
Then Panta's stream with pomp [3] [?] they beset,
East-Saxons' chief and the host from the ships:
No one of them might do harm to the other,   70
But he who by dart's flight his death should receive.
The flood ebbed forth ; the fleetmen stood ready,
Many of wikings, eager for war.
Bade heroes' buckler [4] then hold the bridge
A war-hardened warrior, who Wulfstan was named,   75
Bold 'mid his kin (he was Ceola's son),
Who the first man with his dart shot down
That there most boldly stepped on the bridge.
There stood with Wulfstan warriors fearless,
Ælfhere and Maccus, courageous the twain;   80
At the ford they would nót seek safety in flight,
But firm 'gainst the foes themselves they defended,

---

[1] Money.   [2] Bank of the stream.
[3] *i.e.*, 'battle-array,' Sw., but the word is uncertain; Kr. suggests 'fascines'; Zl. merely gives '*Prunk.*'   [4] *i.e.*, Byrhtnoth.

The while that they weapons were able to wield.
When they that perceived and earnestly saw
That there bridge-fenders [so] fierce they found,   85
Began to lie these loathly guests:
Begged that out-going they might obtain,
Fare o'er the ford, their footmen lead.
Then gan the earl on account of his pride.
Leave too much land to the loathly people   90
Began then to call o'er the water cold
The son [1] of Byrhthelm (the warriors listened):
" Now room is allowed you, come quickly to us,
Warriors to war; wot God aldne
Who this battle-field may be able to keep."   95
Waded the war-wolves, for water they recked not,
The wikings' band, west over Panta,
O'er the clear water carried their shields,
Boatmen to bank their bucklers bore.
There facing their foes ready were standing   100
Byrhtnoth with warriors: with shields he bade
The war-hedge [2] work, and the war-band hold
Fast 'gainst the foes.   Then fight was nigh,
Glory in battle; the time was come
That fated men should there [now] fall.   105
Then out-cry was raised, the ravens circled,
Eagle eager for prey; on earth was uproar.
Then they let from their fists the file-hardened spears,
The darts well-ground, [fiercely] [3] fly forth:
The bows were busy, board point received,   110
Bitter the battle-rush, warriors fell down,
On either hands the youths lay dead.
Wounded was Wulfmaer, death-rest he chose,

[1] i.e., Byrhtnoth.   [2] i.e., the phalanx with interlocked shields.
[3] Some such word as grame, or grimme, seems needed for the alliteration.

Byrhtnoth's kinsman, with bills[1] was hé,
His sister's son, mightily hewn.　　　　　　　　　　115
There was to the wikings recompense given;
Heard I that Edward one of them slew
Strongly with sword, stroke he withheld not,
That fell at his feet the fated warrior;
For that did his prince give thanks to him,　　　　120
To his bower-thane,[2] when he had opportunity.
So firmly stood the fierce-in-mind,
The youths in fight, eagerly thought
Who there with his spear might soonest be able
From a fated man the life to win,　　　　　　　　125
A warrior with weapons: the dead to earth fell.
Steadfast they stood; strengthened them Byrhtnoth,
Bade that each youth of battle should think
He whó on the Danes glory would gain.
Went then a war-brave, his weapon uplifted,　　　130
His shield for defence, and strode towards the chief;
So earnest he went, the earl to the churl:
Each for the other of evil was thinking.
Sent then the seaman his spear from the south
That wounded wás the warrior's lord;　　　　　　135
Then he shoved with his shield that the shaft in two
　　broke,
And the spear was shivered; so sprang it back.
Enraged was the warrior: with his spear he thrust
The wiking proud, who the wound him gave.
Wise was the warrior; he let his spear pierce　　　140
Through the neck of the youth; his hand it guided
So that hé his foe of life deprived.
Then he another speedily shot,
That the byrnie burst; in breast was he wounded

Through the ringèd mail; there stood in his heart   145
The poisonous point.   The earl was the gladder;
Laughed the proud man, to his Maker· gave thanks
For the work of that day that the Lord him gave.
Then let one of warriors a dart from his hands,
Fly from his fist, that forth it went   150
Thróugh that noble thane of Æthelred.
There stood by his side a youth not grown,
A boy in the fight, whó very boldly
Drew from the warrior the bloody spear,
The son of Wulfstan, Wulfmær the young;   155
He let the hard weapon fly. back again;
The point in-pierced, that on earth he lay
Who erst his lord strongly had struck.
Went then an armored man to the earl,
He would the warrior's jewels fetch back,   160
Armor and rings and sword well-adorned.
Then Byrhtnoth drew his sword from its sheath,
Broad and brown-edged, and on byrnie he struck:
Too quickly him hindered one of the seamen,
When he of the earl the arm had wounded;   165
Fell then to earth the fallow-hilt sword:
He might not hold the hardened brand,
His weapon wield.   Yet the word he spake,
The hoary hero the youths encouraged,
Bade forwards go his good companions: 170
He might not on foot longer stand firm;
He looked up to heaven, [the earl exclaimed : [1]]
" I thanks to thee give, Ruler of nations,
For all those joys that on earth I experienced:
Now, Maker mild, most need have I   175
That thou to my spirit the blessing grant,

---

[1] Inserted by Kr. to fill the *lacuna*, whom W. follows; Sw. and Zl. omit.

That my soul to thee may take its course,
Intó thy power, Prince of angels,
With peace may go : I pray to thee,
That fiends of hell may not it harm." 180
Then hewed him down the heathen hinds,
And both the warriors, who by him stood,
Ælfnoth and Wulfmær both lay down dead,
Beside their lord gave up their lives.
Then bowed they from battle who there would not be; 185
There Odda's sons were erst in flight :
From battle went Godric, and the good one forsook,
Who hád on him many a steed oft bestowed :
He leaped on the horse that his lord had owned,
Upon those trappings that right it was not, 190
And his brothers with him both ran away,
Godrinc and Godwig, recked not of war,
But went from the fight, and sought the wood,
Fled to the fastness, and saved their lives,
And more of the men than wás at all meet, 195
If they those services all had remembered,
That he for their welfare to them had done ;
So Offa to him one day had erst said
At the meeting-place, when he held a moot,
That there [very] proudly they many things spake 200
Which after in need they would not perform.[1]
Thén was down-fallen the prince of the folk,
Æthelred's earl : all of them saw,
The hearth-companions, that their lord lay dead.
Then hurried there forth the haughty thanes, 205
The valiant men eagerly hastened :
They would then all the one of the two,
Their lives forsake or their loved one avenge.

---

[1] Lit., 'suffer,' 'endure.'

So urged them ón the son of Ælfric,
A winter-young warrior, with words them addressed, ⌡   210
Then Ælfwine quoth (boldly he spake):
"Remember the times that we oft at mead spake,
When we on the bench our boast upraised,
Heroes in hall, the hard fight anent:
Now may be tested who is the true.[1]   215
I will my lineage to all make known,
That I 'mong the Mercians of mickle race was,
My grandfather wás Ealhhelm by name,
An alderman wise, with wealth endowed.
Ne'er shall 'mong this folk me thanes reproach   220
That I from this host will hasten to wend,
My home to seek, now lies my lord
Down-hewn in fight; to me 'tis great harm:
By blood he was kin and by rank he was lord."[2]
Then went he forth, was mindful of feud,   225
That hé with his spear one of them pierced,
A sailor o' the folk, that he lay on the ground
Killed with his weapon.   Gan he comrades exhort,
Friends and companions, that forth they should go.
Offa addressed them, his ash-spear shook: 230
"Lo! Ælfwine, thóu hast all admonished,
Thanes, of the need.   Now lieth our lord,
Earl on the earth, to us all there is need
That each one of us should strengthen the other
Warrior to war, while weapon he may   235
[Still] have and hold, the hardened brand,
Spear and good sword.   Us hath Godric,
Cowed son of Offa, all [basely] deceived:
So many men thought when on mare he rode,
On thát proud steed, that it wás our lord: 240

---

[1] Lit., 'bold.'   [2] Lit., 'He was both my kinsman and my lord.'

Therefore in field here the folk was divided,
The phalanx broken: may perish his deed,
That he here so many men caused to flee!"
Leofsunu spake, and uplifted his shield,
His buckler for guard; to the warrior he quoth: 245
"I promise thee this, that hence I will nót
A foot's breadth flee, but further will go,
Avenge in battle mine own dear lord.
Me need not 'round Stourmere the steadfast heroes
With words reproach, now my friend has fallen,   250
That, lacking my lord, home I depart,
Wend from the war, but weapons shall take me,
Spear and iron."[1]   Full angry he strode,
Firmly he fought, flight he despised.
Then Dunnere spake, his spear he shook,   255
The agèd churl, called over all,
Bade that each warrior should Byrhtnoth avenge:
"He may not delay who thinks to avenge
His lord on the folk, nor care for his life."
Then forwards they went, they recked not of life;   260
Gan then his followers valiantly fight,
Spear-bearers grim, and to God they prayed,
That théy might avenge their own dear lord,
And upon their foes slaughter fulfil.
Then gan the hostage eagerly help: 265
He was 'mong Northumbrians of valiant race,
The son of Ecglaf, his name was Æscferth:
Ne'er wavered hé in that play of war,
But he hastened forth many a dart;
At times shot on shield, at times killed a chief,   270
Ever and anon inflicted some wound,
The while that he weapon was able to wield.

---

[1] *i.e.*, 'sword.'

Then still in front stood Edward the long,
Ready and eager; boastingly said
That hé would not flee a foot-breadth of land, 275
Backwards withdraw, when his better lay dead:
Broke he the shield-wall and fought 'gainst the war-
 riors,
Till hé his ring-giver upón the seamen
Worthily avenged, ere he lay on the field.
So [too] did Ætheric, noble companion, 280
Ready and eager, earnestly fought he;
Sigebryht's brother and many another
Cleft the curved[1] board, them bravely defended;
Shield's border burst, and the byrnie sang
A terrible song. In battle then slew 285
Offa the seaman that on earth he fell,
And the kinsman of Gadd there sought the ground;
Quickly in battle was Offa hewn down
He had though fulfilled what he promised his lord,
As hé before vowed in face of his ring-giver, 290
That both of them shóuld ride to the borough,
Hale to their homes, or in battle should fall,
Upón the slaughter-place die of their wounds;
He lay like a thane his lord beside.
Then was breaking of boards; the seamen stormed, 295
Enraged by the fight; the spear oft pierced
The fated one's life-house. Forth then went Wigstan,
Son of Thurstan, fought 'gainst the foes:
He wás in the throng the slayer of three,
Ere Wigelin's bairn lay dead on the field. 300
There fierce was the fight: firmly they stood,
Warriors in war, the fighters fell,
Weary with wounds; fell corpses to earth.

---

[1] *i.e.*, 'hollow shields.' *Cellod* is found only here and in Finnsburg, 29.

Oswald and Ealdwald during all the while,
Both of the brothers, emboldened the warriors,   305
Their kinsman-friends bade they in words,
That they in need should there endure,
Unwaveringlý their weapons use.
Byrhtwold [then] spake, uplifted his shield, —
Old comrade was he, — his spear he shook,   310
Hé very boldly exhorted the warriors:
"The braver shall thought be, the bolder the heart,
The more the mood,[1] as lessens our might.
Here lieth our lord, all hewn to pieces,
The good on the ground : ever may grieve   315
Who now from this war-play thinketh to wend.
I am old in years : hence will I not,
But here beside mine own dear lord,
So loved a man, I purpose to lie."
So Æthelgar's bairn them all emboldened,   320
Godric, to battle : oft let he his spear,
His war-spear wind amongst the wikings ;
So 'midst the folk foremost he went,
Hewed he and felled, till in battle he lay ;
This was nót that Godric who fled from the fight.   325

*   *   *   *   *   *   *   *

---

[1] i.e., 'courage.'

www.ingramcontent.com/pod-product-compliance
Lightning Source LLC
Chambersburg PA
CBHW022015050726
47499CB00007BA/2651

9 7 8 3 7 4 4 7 1 9 8 4 1